The Cosmic Embrace
and Other Stories

By Randall DeVallance

For information, or to order additional copies, contact:
Beacon Publishing Group
P.O. Box 41573 Charleston, S.C. 29423
800.817.8480| beaconpublishinggroup.com

Publisher's catalog available by request.

ISBN-13: 978-1-949472-42-4

ISBN-10: 1-949472-42-4

Published in 2022. New York, NY 10001.

First Edition. Printed in the USA.

Contents

The Cosmic Embrace
and Other Stories

The Cosmic Embrace

Tucked into the space between the borders of Turkmenistan, Uzbekistan, Tajikistan, and Afghanistan lies the tiny breakaway province of Hayal Gurunu. This may come as some news to cartographers, not to mention the leaders of each of the four previously mentioned countries, who would insist that their borders press tightly up against one another and that there is simply no room there for a province, breakaway or otherwise. Nevertheless, those same leaders would concede that the region in question is pretty far from their respective capitals and they don't pay a whole lot of attention to what goes on over there, so who knows?

"How big is it?" the President of Uzbekistan asked his advisors. He had just learned of Hayal Gurunu's existence and was none too pleased about it. When told that it was "somewhat smaller than a large town", he shrugged and decided he could live with that. He ordered the State mapmakers to subtract the territory from Tajikistan, as retribution for Scythian atrocities in the 5th Century BC.

Needless to say, this did not go over well in Tajikistan, which felt compelled to point out that the Turkic Khans had hardly been a bunch of girl scouts in their day and ask just where exactly did Uzbekistan get off? The Tajik ambassador to

Uzbekistan went so far as to spill his punch on the carpet during an official reception at the Blue Palace. Tensions flared. No one was in the mood for a war, so the Presidents of both countries arranged a meeting to see if they could come to some sort of agreement. "Look," said the President of Uzbekistan, "why don't we just agree to take it out of Turkmenistan? I mean, *seriously...*" He gave the President of Tajikistan a look.

Turkmenistan, however, was having none of it. "Oh, no you don't!" they said. "We need that land. It's already been zoned."

"For what?" asked Uzbekistan and Tajikistan. "More giant, golden statues of your President?"

"No," said Turkmenistan. "A giant silver statue of a lion standing on the moon. The lion represents the ferocity of our people's spirit, the moon our ambition."

"Ooh," said Uzbekistan and Tajikistan. They had to admit, that sounded pretty cool.

"Look," said Turkmenistan, beckoning the other two countries closer for a quick huddle. After some whispering, they raised their collective heads and turned them to the south.

"You think?" said Tajikistan.

"Do we dare?" said Uzbekistan.

Afghanistan stared back at them, dead-eyed. The other countries gave a start and ducked behind their borders. They were all afraid of Afghanistan. Afghanistan had been getting punched in the face for twenty straight years by the biggest boxing glove on the planet and still refused to yield. America had sent over a trillion dollars' worth of flying death robots to torch every wedding, family reunion, and disco from Badakhshan to Nimruz, and each time Afghanistan would pick itself up off the floor, build a bomb out of a cooking-oil tin and some shoe polish, and blow up a police station. They were as loony as a wedding dress made of razor blades. Afghanistan sat there like an old fighting dog, gnawing on barbed wire and glass shards, waiting for the next country dumb enough to put so much as a toe into its territory.

"On second thought," said Turkmenistan, "what if we just ignore this Hayal Gurunu and go on about our business?"

"Suits me," said Uzbekistan. "I've never even seen Hayal Gurunu."

"Me either," said Tajikistan. "I'm not even sure it exists. Where did it come from, anyway?"

It first appeared, or so its representatives claim, in the early 1990s, when all of Central Asia was in a mad scramble to sort itself out in the wake of the Soviet Union's collapse. One minute there was a mighty Communist empire comprising the northern half of Asia, and the next every group with a claim to an ethnic identity was divvying up the wreckage and cobbling together nations with utilitarian names made up of Turkic and Persian roots. No one was paying much attention to the area around the Panj River, which the founding citizens of Hayal Gurunu claim they were floating down when all the chaos started. They quickly called dibs on the first piece of suitable land they saw.

The problem was, the current was so swift that there was no way to stop their boats. The fledgling Hayal Gurununs were forced to float downriver for several dozen miles before the banks widened and the terrain along the shore flattened enough to provide them with an opportunity to dock. By that time, they could hardly remember where the land they had claimed was.

They abandoned their boats and trudged overland along the riverbank, heading north against the flow of water, certain that when they reached the spot they had chosen for their new homeland they would immediately recognize it and stake their claim. This belief stayed with them throughout the night, began flagging by sunrise, and by midday of the following day – with the desert sun turning their skin the hue and texture of Peking duck – was finally abandoned. Every bend in the river, every boulder or copse of trees they passed looked identical. With the bitter fruit of failure churning in their stomachs and the knowledge of a long journey ahead, they turned and trudged back downriver with the sullen dispositions of teenagers on a family vacation.

The trip back seemed to take twice as long. At first the group attributed this to their weariness and the lack of a big payoff awaiting them at the end. Eventually, however, it occurred to them that they *had* traveled twice as far, and that their boats were nowhere to be seen. Confused, and growing rather desperate now, the group turned as one to its leader – the inimitable Azghibat Gorku, the 'Thundering Hooves', whose lineage was said to trace back to the great steppe chieftains of antiquity – for guidance. Azghibat Gorku stroked his chin solemnly and gazed out into the desert, communing, his followers presumed, with the Great Horse Spirit and the ghosts of his ancestors. After several minutes of silence, during which his followers neither moved nor breathed, he at last turned to face them, a look of easy confidence etched onto his weathered face.

"I think we walked too far," he said.

The group asked if he wouldn't mind repeating himself. He did, and the group – disappointment notwithstanding – had to admit he was probably on to something.

"If we walked too far, why didn't we see the boats?" asked one of the younger followers, whose aversion to physical activity manifested itself in a sort of impudent courage.

Azghibat Gorku was quicker with this one. "We probably weren't paying attention very well."

And with that, the group gathered themselves and once more pivoted one-hundred-and-eighty degrees to begin the march upriver. "Shouldn't we figure out a way to find food?" said one of the women, before they had gone very far. She had only recently joined the group and was still unfamiliar with their ways – for instance, was it normal to go three days without eating, and drinking only tepid river water?

A murmur spread throughout the group, until Azghibat Gorku held up a hand for silence and turned to face them. "The woman speaks truth," he said, apparently under the impression that there was some sort of disagreement on the point, when in fact everyone was starving and on the verge of mutiny. "Remain here. I shall venture into the desert and return laden with fatted meats of such quantity that our children's children shall know not hunger."

"Oh, brother…" said someone in the back.

Histrionics aside, Azghibat Gorku was true to his word. While the rest of the group made camp as best they could with the supplies they had taken from the boats, their leader struck out from the river into the vast wastes surrounding them. He took with him only a *shemagh* and a curved hunting knife worn under his belt, across his stomach in the ceremonial style, though its origin was an Army-Navy Surplus store in Fort Meade, Maryland. They watched him grow increasingly small, his tan robes swallowed up by the sandy horizon, until the moment where – like an image on television when the set is turned off – he seemed to blip out of existence. Then the group turned back toward the river, and each other, to wait.

And wait they did, all through that night into the following morning. A dull rumbling could be heard, not the pounding of horses' hooves against the ground or an earthquake as some first thought, but the collective growling of more than a hundred stomachs protesting their recent treatment. To question the great Azghibat Gorku was unthinkable to most Hayal Gurununs, but hunger and delirium had reverted them to an almost primal state. "Where is that nincompoop?!" they asked. The only response was the howling desert wind.

As the sun sank toward the horizon and another night without food beckoned, the group fell into despair. No more grousing or casual disparagement of Azghibat Gorku was heard; a silence reigned, born of hopelessness. Even the rumbling had faded, as stomach after stomach gave up the struggle.

Like all great legends, it was at this point – when the group's spirits were at their lowest ebb – that a young boy named Izbat sprang to his feet and pointed a finger out into the gloom. "Lookit!" he said.

The group looked. "Ach, boy, it's just a mirage," said the boy's father, Durgum the Skeptical.

"That's no mirage," said Karlov the Contradictory. "It's a shadow."

"Maybe it's a mirage *of* a shadow," said Pashtina the Equivocator.

"I can't see anything!" said Nebald the Nearsighted.

Whatever it was it continued to advance, eventually proving each guesser wrong – it was a person, that much had become clear. But it was also apparent that it was not Azghibat Gorku. Though it wore robes similar to their leader's, the approaching figure lacked his imposing physical presence. It also stumbled a bunch, which was not something one ever saw from the great Son of the Sands (another of Gorku's many titles).

By the time it had staggered to the edge of their camp the tribe could see that it was a man's face beneath the hood, a much whiter (where it was not an angry red) and softer face than they were used to seeing in that part of the world. Likewise, the hands protruding from the ends of the sleeves appeared to the astonished onlookers like a baby's, without crease or callous. The man raised one of these hands in greeting, then immediately lost his balance and lurched to the side, before finding surer footing along the riverbank.

The tribespeople mumbled to one another as the man pressed through the group's outer ranks. Though he spoke no greeting nor gave any command the people parted for him, allowing a respectful distance for him to pass. Although they could not explain it, there was something about the man that compelled the group to defer to him. Perhaps it was the fact that he had clearly never performed a moment's physical labor, which suggested to them a figure of great authority.

The astonished crowd watched as the robed man leapt up onto one of the wide, flat rocks lining the river and stood upon it as if it were a stage, looking down at them with his hands on his hips. "People!" he trumpeted. "Gather round."

The man waited until the group had pressed in close, then reached into the folds of his robe and produced a silver pocket watch dangling from the end of a chain. "Does everyone know what this is?"

The question caused a lot of grumbling amongst the tribe, who resented the implication that just because they spent their time wandering through the desert trying to find where they had left their homeland, they must be the kind of rubes who didn't know a watch when they saw one.

"Ok, ok," said the robed man, raising his hand, "I don't mean to be condescending, it was just a rhetorical flourish. Now, look closely. When the second hand…" he pointed, "… reaches the twelve, I want you to focus all of your attention on it. Follow it closely, blocking out all other distractions, as it makes its journey around the watch face and returns to the number twelve from where it began. Ready? Here it comes…NOW!"

The tribe stared at the watch face, transfixed. Not a sound could be heard but the gurgling of the Panj behind them, the distant moan of the desert winds, and the incessant "tick-tick-tick" of the second hand as it embarked on its revolution, past the three, dipping down to touch the six, then beginning the long climb up past the nine, ten, and eleven to once again summit at twelve.

No sooner had the second hand reached its destination than the group leaned back as one, as if released from a spell they had all been under.

"Now," said the robed man, "what did we learn?"

The tribe members turned their heads left and right, searching their neighbors' faces to see if they were the only ones who had no idea what the point of the exercise was supposed to be.

"I'll tell you what we learned," said the robed man, a moment later. The tribe members breathed a sigh of relief. *"Being rhetorical,"* one of them murmured to anyone nearby who was listening.

"What we learned," said the robed man, "is that I just wasted a minute of your time."

There was a pause, during which there was much squinting and scrunching of faces. Finally, one woman's eyes went wide. "Hey, he's right!"

A hubbub spread throughout the group, equal parts incredulity and outrage at the trick that had been played on them. The robed man looked on in silence, tight-lipped as he waited for the tumult to reach its crescendo. Finally, he stretched out an arm, his open hand hovering over their heads as if to anoint them, and bellowed, "People!"

The chatter died down, then stopped altogether as the assembled faces focused once more on the robed man. "This is what the world is doing to you every day," he said. "Stealing your time as they tell you to stare at their watches."

"Or clocks!" someone shouted.

"Or clocks, that's exactly right." The robed man slipped the watch back into his pocket and began pacing the length of the rock. "That is what I've come here to tell you about. That is what I have made it my *mission* to impart to you – the knowledge

10

and the wisdom to start living life according to your own clock. Ladies and gentlemen…" Stopping in the center of the rock, he reached down to untie the rope cinched around his waist, then grasped the front of his robe and threw it open to reveal a bespoke suit of the finest silk and Italian calfskin wingtips. "My name is Radislav Zulitsky. And the thing I have come all this way to tell you about is…the Zulitsky Method!"

There was a shocked silence, followed soon after by a dumbfounded silence, which gradually morphed into an awkward, embarrassed silence. Zulitsky gazed down at them, a look of triumph plastered on his face that showed no signs of waning. The group milled about for a bit, until finally Beghnir the Brave shouldered his way to the front and raised his hand. "Huh?" he said.

"That's the name," said Zulitsky. "The secrets that will let you live life according to your own clock. I named it after myself."

"Ah," said the group.

"Well," said Beghnir, "that sounds like a pretty valuable thing you're selling. I guess that minute we spent staring at your watch wasn't such a waste of time after all."

Zulitsky gave a slight bow.

"Hold on," said a woman named Aliye, who at the time had no honorific, but from that day forward would be known to the tribe as Aliye the Analytical. "If the lesson was valuable, then the minute we spent staring at your watch wasn't a waste of time. Which contradicts the point you were trying to make, and therefore in retrospect renders the lesson worthless. But if the lesson is worthless, then the minute we spent staring at your watch was worthless, which in itself validates the lesson…"

"Go on," said Zulitsky.

"But if the lesson is validated, then it ceases to be worthless!" said Aliye.

"People, people! This is exactly the sort of conundrum the Zulitsky Method was designed to untangle." With a magician's flourish, Zulitsky hopped down from the rock, giving no thought to what the sand might do to his Italian shoes as he moved amongst the group like a true man of the people. "Imagine," he said, "lying on your death bed and looking back at this moment, the time and energy that was expended trying to unravel what in the end is a meaningless paradox." He paused and looked around at the gathered faces, eyebrow raised. "Does anyone here believe they'll be thinking to themselves, *I wish I had spent more time mulling over that stupid question?*"

Toward the fringes of the group a hand started to go up, until someone nearby whispered, "*Rhetorical!*", after which it slowly lowered again.

"The Zulitsky Method will provide you with the tools needed to break life's chains," said Zulitsky. "The chains that keep us obsessing over problems that don't matter." The crowd murmured its agreement. "Telling ourselves we aren't 'good enough'." Zulitsky made air quotes around the words 'good enough', earning some heartfelt whoops of approval. "Keeping us from realizing our dreams and attaining the happiness that's right there in front of us, waiting to be plucked like apples from a tree!" The crowd began to cheer, then trailed off; having lived their entire lives in a desert region they had never seen an apple tree.

"But what *is* it?" asked Zeyneb the Clarifier.

"It's a whole new way of looking at the world," said Zulitsky. "It is a seismic shift in the global paradigm, a roadmap for actualizing the un-actualizable. It is simplicity in a complicated age."

"Golly," said the crowd. Only Elgbar the Shameless looked confused. "I don't get it," he said, earning some withering looks from the others.

Zulitsky sucked in a breath and released it in a slow, even stream. The Zulitsky Method, he explained, promotes communion, understanding, and the spiritual properties of the flesh as embodied in the hug, which in Zulitsky's teachings was the symbolic recreation by two individuals of the circular universe we inhabit. When two people hug, they create a gravitational force that draws in "positive ions" from the surrounding space-time fabric, a claim with which physicists would surely have quibbled had there been any within a hundred-mile radius to hear it. Needless to say, continued Zulitsky, the Presidents of the countries in the region were very much opposed to hugs, which is why his presence there was so critical.

The Zulitsky Method also held that for self-development it was important for people to release negative energy. Sharing a hug with someone with too much pent-up negative energy could create an emotional-spiritual black hole, drawing in heavier negative ions from the space-time fabric that could drag both parties down into a deep depression. Wouldn't the positive ions also be drawn in, you might ask? Yes, but the negative ions are bigger, Zulitsky would respond, crowding out the positive ions and creating a net-negative effect. Question further and Zulitsky would point out that neither you nor he is a scientist, which almost always turned out to be the case.

"So…" said Zeyneb, "you want us to hug each other?"

"The only thing I need you to do right now," said Zulitsky, laying his hand on her shoulder, "is follow me."

And with that he was off, striding north along the banks of the Panj with the cocksure swagger of a runway model. Having wandered aimlessly for so many days, the sight of a man heading in a definite direction was too enticing for the Hayal Gurununs to resist. After a moment's pause, a mad scramble began in which everyone rushed to gather their belongings and scamper after their new Prophet-King, for that's what Zulitsky had become in fact if not yet in name. Not a thought was spared for poor Azghibat Gorku, the 'Thundering Hooves', who for all his people knew was still trudging through the desert looking for an antelope to club over the head.

****

The planet Ryball VII is very different from Earth. For one thing, it orbits two suns instead of one, weaving through them in a continuous figure-eight pattern. You would think this would make Ryball VII a terribly hot planet on which to live, but as each sun emits only half the heat of the Earth's, things pretty much even out in the end.

The planet also has a strange way of rotating, constantly changing direction as if lacking a fixed axis. The effect, when paired with the double suns, is that both day and night on Ryball VII seem to last for weeks, while at the same time ending before they even have a chance to begin. Yet somehow, over the course of a lifetime the average Ryballian spends almost fifty percent of its life in sunlight and the other fifty percent in darkness. Once again, things find a way to even out.

"It all evens out in the end" is the planetary motto of Ryball VII. This has nothing to do with temperature or daylight, nor is it a general philosophical precept, but refers instead to cake frosting. An interesting side effect of Ryball VII's complex gyrations is that no matter how one applies frosting to a cake, the planetary movements ensure a smooth finish. This has brought a great deal of prosperity to Ryball VII as a galactic hub for cake decorating, and is why the inhabitants of neighboring star systems refer to it as "God's Icing Turntable".

There are fourteen moons orbiting Ryball VII. When added to the planet's irregular rotation – which causes the stars one sees in the sky on any given night to be entirely different than those from the previous night – a cosmography so complex is created that a significant portion of the population are employed full-time as astrologers. "If you don't like your luck, just wait a smektar," goes a popular phrase on Ryball VII. A "smektar" is the Ryballian word for "hour", which is equivalent to somewhere between five Earth weeks and 0.357 Earth seconds, depending on which way the planet happens to be spinning at that moment. Fortunes change so quickly on Ryball VII that the planet's wealthiest inhabitant might find himself the poorest by early evening, or vice versa, though perhaps unsurprisingly Ryballians experience some of the lowest levels of income inequality in the universe over the long term.

Trying to describe what a typical inhabitant of Ryball VII looks like is a fool's errand, since Ryballians tend to adopt the appearance of the dominant species on whatever planet they visit. This is not a conscious choice, but an autonomic response. Ryballians are so bashful and generally down on themselves that their brains automatically release chemicals into the body ordering it to blend in with the local population. Therefore, the best answer to the question, "What does a Ryballian look like?", is, "you and me", which holds true no matter to whom you are speaking.

Only on Ryball VII itself can one encounter Ryballians in their natural form. Unfortunately, given the aforementioned planetary gyrations almost no one can undertake such a visit without becoming violently ill. (Extended visits often lead to madness.) Ryballians themselves describe their appearance as being something between a sand crab and head lice, though larger and – Ryballians are quick to stress – with nicer complexions.

Not long ago, Ryballians were about as engaging as sand crabs. Like all complex organisms the Ryballians evolved from a simpler species, but the speed and method of their evolution was like no other. Early Ryballians, as is typical of primitive lifeforms, were preoccupied mainly with finding food. This task can be difficult enough in ideal conditions, but nearly impossible on a planet that moves like a malfunctioning carnival ride. The ever-shifting rotation made simple movement across the planet's surface a feat worthy of an Olympic gymnast. Many early Ryballians succumbed to starvation, stumbling around the planet trying to grab hold of a glibnorb root (a Ryballian delicacy, sort of like a beet) or a beet (native to Ryball VII, and also considered a delicacy).

Certain Ryballians found that by extending their pincers and clutching on to one of their fellow citizens, they could create a wider base that improved their balance and allowed them to navigate the world well enough to survive. Thus did the centrality of the hug to Ryballian culture take root.

While this was going on, the torque from the planet's abrupt changes in direction was so intense that Ryballians' skulls began to stretch, providing additional space for the expansion of their brains. Over a span of ten generations the intelligence of the average Ryballian increased a thousand-fold. The added skull space also allowed for new lobes to develop that better calibrated their nervous systems to their planet's anti-gyroscopic tendencies. No longer were Ryballians forced to grab onto their neighbor's shoulders (carapace, really) in order to get around. And yet, rather than fade away, the practice of hugging persisted, taking on a religious significance within the culture. The simplicity of the circle formed by hugging stood in contrast to the complexity of Ryball VII's celestial pinballing, and seemed to make for a neat metaphor about the importance of togetherness. To the hug did Ryballians owe their species' rapid ascendancy.

Even now, when the dimmest Ryballian is on par with the greatest of Earth's thinkers, it is a common belief among them that the hug possesses mystical powers, the full extent of which they are only beginning to understand. Whether this is a holdover belief from their primitive days, too deeply ingrained now to excise, or something based in fact is a hotly debated topic. When the schism first developed it was assumed that time would bring the answers, a not unreasonable assumption given the exponential growth in Ryballians' intelligence up to that point. "Our grandchildren will be laughing at us," was a common sentiment at the time, as most assumed that brain size would expand enough over the next few generations to make child's play of the problem. However, the same developments that improved the Ryballians' balance also lessened the effect of the planet's torque on their skulls, impeding further growth. By the time those hypothetical grandchildren were born Ryballian intelligence had plateaued, and the divide over the divinity of the hug had become a conflict as intractable as Catholic vs. Protestant, Sunni vs. Shia.

This theological disagreement was the reason that a pair of Ryballians, Xyghitix Florp and Kleinmerp Bazzlewind, had traveled several million lightyears to check into room 112 of the Silk Road Motel Bar & Lounge in Tashkent, Uzbekistan under the aliases "Rick Everyman" and "Joe Average". As Senior Adherents in the High Church of the Embrace, one of their main tasks on Ryball VII involved a combination of missionary work and scientific research intended to prove once and for all that hugs were the key to unlocking creation's greatest mysteries. Their work spanned several galaxies and included thousands of planets, but one of the earliest test sites (and a sentimental favorite of Florp's and Bazzlewind's) was Earth, chosen both because the human anatomy is well-designed for administering hugs and because of its vast distance from Ryball VII. Hug-worshipers believed that the more far-flung and distinct the civilization was from Ryball VII, the stronger the case would be for a unified theory putting hugs at the center of the universe's machinations.

For thousands of years, High Church observers had monitored the evolution of the human race and extrapolated the importance of hugs to its development, utilizing a network of trillions of tiny cameras scattered across the planet (a sophisticated and expensive bit of technology that the Ryballians were only able to afford thanks to their vast cake-decorating fortune, and which humans referred to, rather charmingly, as "bees").

The results seemed largely to bear out the High Church's claims. Hugs had been identified at the juncture of many momentous occurrences throughout Earth's history. For instance, it was noted that Johannes Gutenberg had received an affectionate squeeze from his Aunt Hilda just days before inventing the printing press. Monet hugged no less than seven different women during the painting of *Water Lilies*. This was all to the good.

There was, however, a disturbing bent to some of their observations, even as they seemed to further confirm the High Church's central tenet. Though humans had been hugging for longer and with greater frequency than just about any other species in the known universe, they also happened to be spectacularly, unabashedly violent. To a species like the Ryballians – for whom violence was such a foreign concept that their planet's legal framework included no provisions forbidding it – this aspect of human behavior was a riddle without answer. Questions like, "Why is that man poking that other man with a sharp, metal object?" gave way over the years to, "Why is that man propelling tiny, lead cylinders at a considerable velocity into that other man's torso?", but answers remained just as elusive.

The debate over what to make of this paradox led to a further rift within the High Church, between those who viewed the hug as an unambiguous force for good and the "Amoralists", who believed that hugs were simply a power source that could be used toward any end, good or bad. The Amoralists pointed to Napoleon's marital embrace of the Empress Josephine just days before his smashing of Habsburg forces in Italy, or the several birthday hugs Richard Gatling received before inventing the self-contained, reloadable steel cylinders and independent firing mechanism that led to the machine gun. Consequential developments both, but resulting in a lot more poking and propelling of lead cylinders than the Moralist's worldview would seem to support.

It was against this backdrop that Florp and Bazzlewind made a startling discovery one afternoon while scanning the day's surveillance footage from Earth. A bee in the Central Asia region had stumbled across a man espousing a philosophy he called the "Zulitsky Method". Not only did this philosophy center around the spiritual properties of the hug, but it included a workable theory for why certain hugs led to negative outcomes. It was a potentially monumental development, promising not only to give the High Church the ammunition it needed to win the day over its rationalist opposition, but providing a framework that could bridge the gap between its Moralist and Amoralist factions.

With great excitement, Florp and Bazzlewind brought news of their discovery to their shift supervisor, the Archdeacon Torkwhistle Spinoza.

"*Negative ions*," breathed Spinoza. "Why didn't we think of that?"

"Probably because our brains aren't big enough," said Florp. "We're so dumb."

"Frightfully dumb," said Spinoza. "I'm surprised we even understand it now that someone's pointed it out for us."

"Um…to be honest guys, I still kind of don't get it," said Bazzlewind.

"You either?" Spinoza wiped his forehead. "Phew! I thought I was the only one. God, we're the worst."

"The absolute worst!" said Florp.

"There's only one thing for it," said Spinoza.

"You don't mean…?" said Bazzlewind.

Spinoza nodded. "You two are going to have to travel to Earth and speak with this Zulitsky fellow. Find out whatever he can teach us about these negative ions."

"If he'll even agree to talk to us," said Florp, sulkily.

"Well, that's always a concern," said Spinoza. "We are frightfully tedious creatures. But that's a risk we're going to have to take. The stakes are too high."

"Do you really think we're the right ones for the job?" said Bazzlewind. "A couple of yo-yos like us?"

"Who knows more about Earth culture than you two?" said Spinoza. "I'll bet you already know what disguises you're going to wear."

"Well…" said Florp, going a bit blue in the shell (the Ryballian form of blushing). "There are a few ideas that come to mind, actually."

"I expected no less," said Spinoza, proudly. "We're a sorry bunch, but you're the best we've got for the job at hand. I expect you'll embarrass us less than you think."

Bazzlewind blinked back a tear. "Thanks, boss."

"Now listen," said Spinoza, "take the rest of the day off and go home, make the necessary arrangements. Earth is in the Milky Way, on the far side of the Andromeda galaxy. We're talking five or six million lightyears here, so the trip's going to take at least a couple hours each way."

Florp and Bazzlewind groaned. "Maybe the Earthlings can teach us a halfway decent mode of intergalactic transportation while they're at it."

"One miracle at a time," said Spinoza. He stood at attention, like a great Earth General sending his charges into battle. "The High Church is counting on you boys. Make your old Archdeacon proud."

With that, he extended his pincers – Florp and Bazzlewind doing likewise – and the three figures encircled one another in a solemn embrace.

****

As soon as the encampment was out of view, Azghibat Gorku craned his neck to make sure no one had followed him and then began frantically looking around for something to stab. The sun that only hours before had been a blistering white pinprick directly above them – as if God were a sadistic child with a magnifying glass burning insects – had now become a red ball dipping toward the horizon. Gorku huddled within his robes, no longer to protect his skin but to stave off the chill brought on by the increasingly intense breezes blowing in from the deep desert. As he tromped through the sand, he muttered to himself: "Idiot...stupid idiot...you stupid, stupid idiot...dumb idiot...you stupid, dumb idiot...dumbass...you dumbass idiot...you stupid, dumb, stupid dumdum idiot...dumb head..." and so on.

He had calculated wrong. American movies, which had recently begun flooding the region following the collapse of Communism, had taught him that in times of trouble the leader of a beleaguered people should announce his intention to venture alone into the maw of certain death. This in turn should rouse several of the strongest men in the group – as well as one extremely fit, attractive woman who has no time for outmoded gender roles and isn't afraid to mix it up with the boys – to raise a rallying cry and charge after him into the breach. Not for the first time, reality had failed to live up to Hollywood's high ideals.

Gorku scanned the barren landscape, hoping for any signs of movement. He was fooled several times by the shifting sands, which the breeze made wriggle back and forth like an animal weaving its way through the dunes. If he were lucky, he might spot an antelope or gazelle. They rarely came so far south, but it was not an impossible scenario. He pictured himself striding into camp, a dead antelope draped across his shoulders like a milkmaid's yoke, to a hero's welcome. Unfortunately, his imagination was unable to fill in the events between that happy scene and the moment when he first spotted the antelope, assuming such a thing were to occur. As cinematic as it was marching into the desert with only a knife strapped to one's belt, it was poor survival preparation.

The best strategy Gorku had come up with to subdue his prey was to sneak up behind it, tiptoeing across the sand (in his mind this tiptoeing was accompanied by a tinkling piano, like in a Looney Tunes short), and leap upon its back like a professional wrestler administering a sleeper hold. This plan was even worse than Gorku understood it to be, and he was hardly optimistic about its success.

The nickname "Thundering Hooves" had been given to him by his tribe not because of his horse-riding prowess or because of his willingness to charge into battle like a herd of wild mustangs, but because he had just about the loudest footsteps any of them had ever heard. Many a visit from the great leader had been prefaced by a clomping sound that sent shudders through the walls of their yurts. Even when crossing the sand his footsteps seemed to reverberate like a man in work boots stomping across a creaky wooden floor. A proverb held that when Thundering Hooves comes to visit even Feruza the Deaf puts out cookies. Gorku had always considered this to be a comment on his larger-than-life stature, that one could practically sense his presence as he approached, but Feruza swore up and down that she could hear his big, lead hoofers stomping up the path to her home a full minute before he actually showed up. It was a mark of the tribe's respect for Gorku that they had kept these things hidden from him throughout the years, which meant that for his entire life had had remained blissfully unaware that he was – quite literally – a walking punchline.

Nevertheless, Gorku saw plenty of other problems with the options available to him. For one, he had never killed an animal before. This may be a surprising thing to learn about the chief of a nomadic tribe, but remember that by that point Hayal Gurunu had existed for only a couple of weeks. Before that Gorku and the rest of his tribe had lived in a tiny, Soviet mining town on the Kazakh steppe, sifting bauxite out of the topsoil to ship to Boksitogorsk so it could be turned into aluminum. The town was hundreds of miles from where any of them had grown up, but Moscow had given them their marching orders, and so they had packed up their families and relocated in the name of Soviet prosperity. Gorku was made a foreman at the mine, seemingly at random. His days had consisted mainly of wandering around the dig site making small talk with his subordinates, reading the paper in his office, and drinking in the smoke-filled village bar with the other men until after dark. Every day he ate his lunch at a café across the street from the mine's entrance. He had never been hunting in his life.

Gorku was pretty certain that if he had a gun, or even a bow and arrow, he could bring himself to kill for food. The distance a projectile weapon created between hunter and prey cushioned the psyche, allowing him to construct a narrative that it had not really been him who had been responsible for taking the animal's life. Knives, on the other hand, allowed no room for self-deception. Even if he somehow overcame his sonorous footfalls and subpar speed and managed to leap upon an antelope's back, what then? Could he take his knife and draw the blade across the poor thing's throat, or plunge it through the back of its neck? Just the thought made him queasy. But another day without food might change the calculus. Even the most refined man is only a few missed meals from becoming a savage.

As the sun dipped lower and the sands turned from red to black, Gorku wandered the dunes without plan or direction, putting his trust in dumb luck. Any thought of antelope or gazelle had been shelved.

There would be no feasting at the camp tonight. He now hoped for anything he could bring back, no matter how small, to give his people hope that the Great Spirits had not forsaken them altogether.

Dusk was when the desert came alive. Gorku shook off his increasing exhaustion and kept his eyes peeled for hares or hedgehogs. *Even a jerboa would do*, he thought. Atop a rocky ridge not far from where he stood, a steppe eagle stared at him impassively. The breeze continued to blow, the shifting sands now resembling snakes, much to Gorku's discomfort.

Several times he considered turning back, but the thought of returning to his people empty-handed prevented him. He played out every permutation of the scene in his head, picturing himself breaking the news to his followers that there would once again be nothing to eat that evening. None of the scenarios ended well. At best, the news would be accepted with a quiet resignation that did nothing to lessen the suffering apparent on the people's faces. At worst, he himself became dinner. No matter what, his reputation would suffer. And so he pushed on, always with the hope that over the next dune he would find the answer to his prayers.

Hours passed. Enough dunes had been crested that Gorku was no longer sure he could find his way back to the encampment, whether or not he found food. Any familiar landmarks had long since been left behind. All around him was sand, rising and falling in undulations as anonymous as ocean swells. What's more, the sun had dropped below the horizon, plunging the world into near-total darkness; only the silvery light of a half-moon gave Gorku anything to go by. A gnawing fear took hold in the back of his mind that, once ensconced, began to feed off of itself. In an effort to reassure himself that he wasn't lost, he turned around and began tracing his footsteps back the way he had come. However, the footprints were difficult to see in the dim light, and by the time he had backtracked to the top of the dune immediately behind him he was dismayed to see that the wind had all but erased them. Further on, no doubt, they had already vanished. It was then that the scope of his mission changed, from returning to his tribe a conquering hero to surviving the night.

Gorku pulled his robes tightly around him. They were made of a loose, light fabric, designed to protect from the sun and allow air to circulate. Now, with the sun down and the temperature plunging, they became a liability. The wind worked its way through every opening, crawling up and down his skin like centipedes made of ice. In the beginning it spurred him to walk faster, physical exertion being the only thing that managed to keep his temperature up. But with no food or water it was impossible to keep up a steady pace. The harder he pushed forward the more exhausted he became, which caused his pace to slow and the cold to once more tighten its grip.

He knew he needed to bed down somewhere and wait for morning. Circling the nearest dune until he reached its leeward side, he knelt and began digging a trench along its base. Eventually, he managed to form a narrow crevice and wormed his way inside. Though it was not deep enough to cover him completely, it did protect from the wind. Bunching his robes in front of him, he huddled within his makeshift shelter and hoped his body heat would be enough to keep him alive through the night.

The next thing Gorku knew he was being strangled to death. Not strangled – suffocated. He tried to breathe in and gagged. A weight pressed down on his chest. His throat felt constricted and burned whenever he gasped for air, as if he had inhaled a plume of smoke. Panic rose within him, and his survival instincts kicked in. He wriggled his arms and legs, fueled by a rush of adrenaline. Whichever way he tried to move he felt resistance, as if he were swaddled in a straightjacket. Still, he clawed and punched and thrashed, until at last he felt a part of the barrier give way and his hand thrust out into the open air beyond. Forcing his other hand through the opening, he dug his fingers into the sand outside and pulled, kicking with his legs like a swimmer propelling himself along the water's surface. Gorku felt as if his head were a balloon being squeezed to its bursting point, until all at once clean, crisp air rushed in to fill the space around him. He lay on the ground, inhaling greedily between hacking coughs as his lungs tried to expel the dust that had collected there.

Minutes later, after his fits had subsided and his heart rate had begun to slow, Gorku dragged himself forward to free his legs, then rolled over and sat up. Where his shelter had been, only a tiny indentation remained. He must have fallen asleep immediately after lying down, he reasoned, after which the dune had shifted and covered him in sand. A shiver passed through him, not from the cold this time but from the fate he had narrowly escaped. Had the wind blown differently and the dune collapsed, he would have been buried so deeply he could never have dug himself out. There were many ways to die, but few worse that Gorku could think of than being entombed in a mountain of sand.

It dawned on him that he could see the dune and the remnants of his shelter clearly. The sun was already peeking above the eastern horizon; he must have been asleep for hours, he realized. He climbed to the top of the next dune and stood there, feeling the sunlight soak into his aching muscles and chase the chill from his bones. The warmth and the rest he had gotten the night before buoyed his spirits, made him forget for a moment how precarious his situation was. Even his hunger pangs had subsided, like a roaring fire that had burned through all its fuel. His thirst, however, was worse than ever. Without water he would not survive another day, and the sun that now brought him so much comfort would in a few hours become his tormentor.

Methodically, he searched the sky for circling birds. Finding none, he looked around him, checking the near and middle distance for insects – flies, mosquitos, anything that might gather around a source of moisture – but in his delirium every shadow or cloud of sand carried by the wind looked like an insect swarm. No vegetation could be seen anywhere. Scanning the horizon, he saw what he thought looked like a rocky area to his northeast. He started off in that direction, hoping to find a shady canyon or old river bed that might have retained some moisture from whenever the last rains had been. He moved slowly to avoid working up a sweat, but steadily, aware always of the sun that even now buffeted the side of his face through his raised hood.

The journey took all of the morning and into the afternoon. Gorku understood the tricks a wide, flat expanse could play on the mind when trying to judge distances. Even so, he was dismayed that each time he raised his eyes from the sand to check his progress the rocks seemed to be no closer than when he had first spotted them. The thought flickered through his mind that perhaps they were not really there at all, were just a mirage, but he quickly dismissed it – not because he was sure it wasn't true, but because his sanity depended on it. Hopelessness was the enemy now, and delusion – insofar as it kept him moving and fighting – had become his ally. He trudged on, one step at a time, focusing on the ground in front of him and looking up only to ensure that he was still pointed in the right direction.

By the time he was close enough to know for sure that the rocks were real, the sun was high overhead. Its beams pressed down on his back and shoulders like a giant hand trying to pin him to the ground. A few times he nearly did pitch forward onto his face, but at the last second managed to find his footing. Gorku knew he couldn't afford to fall. The sand at that time of day could blister skin as surely as a hot stovetop. Though he lurched and stumbled, he managed to maintain his balance as his thoughts turned always to water. When Gorku finally reached the base of the first outcrop, the shade it cast enveloped him like a cool bath. Yet for all the relief it provided, he could think only of getting to higher ground. If there was any moisture to be found it would be there, amongst the high rocks. He only hoped the topography would cooperate.

The climb was long and arduous, made all the more difficult by the fact that it required Gorku to leave the comfort of his current position and put himself once more in the path of the sun's rays. The rock face where he stood was too steep for a direct ascent. He circled the base until the formation began to flatten and widen. A pile of loose boulders and smaller rocks offered footholds that allowed him to get started, though even this initial push felt as if it took every ounce of strength his body possessed.

At the top of the pile, the ground leveled off. Gorku hoisted himself up and saw with some dismay that he had climbed no more than ten feet off the ground. The area where he now stood was the edge of a sweeping expanse that formed the northern base of the outcrop. Above him loomed the peak, not three-hundred feet tall at its highest point, though to Gorku it may as well have been Mount Everest he was looking at. The northern approach was less severe than the cliffs he had first encountered to the south, but offered no easy way to the top. What's more, there were no obvious depressions further up that looked as if they might hold a significant amount of water.

Gorku walked the perimeter of the base, looking down over the edge for any crevices that might have formed to trap runoff from above, but the sand uniformly pressed up against the rock's edge. In the distance were more outcroppings, dozens of them jutting into the sky, some far bigger than the one on which he now stood. He considered abandoning his current position and trying his luck elsewhere, but the next closest formation was more than a mile away. He knew he would never have the strength to climb the rocks even if he were able to make it there. There was nothing to do but climb and hope for the best.

The path Gorku picked out wound back and forth, a series of switchbacks that lost elevation nearly as much as they gained. Each time he reached the edge of the formation and was forced to backtrack, he stopped to rest. At first it was only for a few minutes each time, but by the time he had reached the midway point of his ascent he seemed to be resting more than moving. It was all he could do on the occasions he chose to sit down to drag himself to his feet again when it came time to press on.

He had no idea how long he had been at it. The sun was now well past its zenith and falling in the western sky. A small mercy, though one Gorku was hard-pressed to appreciate. His condition was deteriorating. The skin on his face clung to his skull, and his tongue was swollen and numb. Strange specters flitted past on the edges of his vision – snakes, demons, and other grotesque images that made him start and clench up in fear, before turning his head to find that there was nothing there. *Well*, he thought to himself, *that's just great.*

Somewhere above he could hear a rhythmic tapping, just audible beneath the ever-present moan of the wind. He tuned it out while he measured the distance to the next switchback. Auditory hallucinations were the least of his worries. He reached a small gap in the ledge he was crossing and leaped over it. Though narrow enough that a child could have hopped back and forth over it for hours, the energy he expended to do so just once left him exhausted. He staggered back against the rock face before crumpling to the ground, wondering if he could will himself to get up just one more time and continue on.

The tapping noise continued above him, unabated. In fact, it had grown louder. It seemed to be directly above his head now. Unable to move or even open his eyes for more than a few seconds, he sat back against the rocks and listened as he tried to gather his strength. What had seemed a rather flat, dull sound before had changed in pitch. There was a "plinking", echoey quality to it, like water dripping into a pool.

Water.

Gorku's eyes snapped open and he leapt to his feet as if he had only been napping a moment. Behind him was a section of sheer cliff terminating at the top in another ledge like the one he now stood on. Gorku estimated it to be around eight feet tall. He stretched his hands up as high as he could, but was still a foot or more from being able to grasp the edge.

He moved back a step and studied the path he was on. If he continued following the same ledge all the way to the eastern end of the formation, it looked as though there was a switchback that would bring him up to the ledge above, where he could then retrace his steps west until he reached the source of the sound. It was not a short journey. At his current pace it might take him hours to complete the circuit. Gorku wasn't sure how much time he had left. All the while, the "drip-drip-drip" sound continued, like a siren's call. He started off on the path he had laid out, picking his way over rocks and other obstacles, but found himself slowing as the dripping sound faded in the background. That sound meant hope to him, and he could not leave it behind – no matter how necessary – without feeling that all was lost.

Gorku studied the cliff face from a distance and could see now that it was not perfectly flat. All up and down its surface were irregularities, small fissures and protrusions that potentially offered some grip. If he could get up high enough to grab the ledge with his hands, he might be able to use them as footholds and pull himself up the rest of the way.

Even in his head it sounded farfetched, but as he returned to the spot and the dripping sound grew audible once again it went from an idle thought to a compulsion. He could not bear to leave, not when he was so close. This would be his last stand. He would find a way to pull himself up or die trying.

He found the place where the dripping was at its loudest and stood with his chest and palms pressed flat against the cliff, staring straight up at the ledge above him. He lifted a foot and tested the surface of the rock with his boots, finding a spot where the treads seemed to catch and offered him a place to push off from. Unfortunately, his fingers could find no purchase; he groped the rockface above him for something to hold on to, feeling his life wane with every wasted movement. Still, the ledge beckoned, taunting him.

A surge of anger rose up within him. With a rasping cry the great Thundering Hooves bent his knees and leapt upward with every ounce of strength left in his body. As his fingertips closed over the top of the ledge, he felt a momentary sensation of wetness against his parched, splintered skin. *Water,* he thought. A moment later, the stone beneath his fingers crumbled and gave way. Azghibat Gorku plummeted like a lead canary, crashing onto the ledge below.

Lights danced in front of his eyes, and he arched his back in pain. It was as if someone had filled his veins with gasoline and dropped in a lit match. The shock of the impact erased whatever determination remained within him. As the initial wave of agony began to subside, he wanted nothing more than to rest, to close his eyes and drift away from this place forever and ever. He lay there like a discarded children's toy, head lolled back over the edge of the cliff as he stared out at the desert, inverted now, endless miles of sand and rock stretching out beyond the horizon above him while below was only a cloudless, blue void.

A sense of peace he hadn't felt since first setting out from the mines all those weeks ago enveloped him, and he smiled, despite the lingering pain. He blinked his eyes, focusing on a point far out across the sand. It almost looked to him as if something was moving out there. He blinked again, slower and longer this time, suffused with the bliss of absolute surrender. There was nothing more to fight for. No reason to be afraid.

His eyes drooped shut for several seconds, then opened again. The moving object was closer this time. Gorku could see that it was a vehicle of some sort, like a chariot, spewing clouds of sand in its wake as it sped toward him. Once more his eyelids fell, washing away the thirst that had become his constant companion. Though he wanted nothing more than to leave them shut forever, he could not resist taking a final look at the apparition that was approaching.

The vehicle had passed the next-closest rock formation now and was barreling toward him across the open desert. On its back stood a woman in gleaming white robes that rippled in the wind, her red hair streaming out behind her like an arc of flame. Though nearly a mile away her eyes seemed to be locked onto Gorku's. *The Old Woman of the Desert,* he thought. Soon he would be meeting his ancestors on the plains of Uçmag.

The woman raised her arm and leveled a finger at Gorku. He smiled and let his eyes close once and for all, as he waited for the darkness to carry him away.

****

When Gorku opened his eyes again, his first thought was that Heaven was not at all like he'd expected.

It was itchier, for one. The sheets that covered him were stiff and scratchy, like cheap hospital linens. He was lying on a bed, inside a tent of some sort. The canvas was aglow, infused with golden light. That felt appropriate, if not the broader idea of finding a tent in the afterlife. He squirmed, trying to get comfortable and frowning at the creaking of the springs that dug into his back through a lumpy, feather mattress. *Itches in Heaven,* he thought. *Who would have guessed?*

Unless...

He gasped and sat up as if he'd been pricked with a pin, sending his sheets fluttering onto the floor. At the same time a flap at the far end of the tent opened and the Old Woman of the Desert entered. At least, Gorku thought it was her. Her hair was not so much a billowing flame as copper-colored, slightly wavy and pulled back into a loose ponytail. Instead of white robes she wore khaki pants and a matching button-down shirt, like an extra in an *Indiana Jones* movie. In her hand she held a glass of water. She smiled.

"Am I in Hell?" said Gorku.

She stared at him for a moment. "Just what every woman hopes to hear when she walks into a room." She shook her head and came further into the tent, placing the water on a table next to his bed. "You sound like a Saudi prince. I didn't realize nomads were so particular about their accommodations."

She remained by his bedside, looking down at him with a curious expression. Gorku frowned. "You're no goddess," he said.

"And you're no Paul Newman." Her gaze broke from his and migrated downward, her eyes growing wide. "But I suppose I can overlook it."

Gorku looked down and realized he was naked. He scrambled to retrieve his sheets from the floor, wincing at the pain that rippled up and down his back. *My back.* As if recalling something that had happened to him in another lifetime, an image of him plummeting from the side of a cliff flashed through Gorku's mind.

"Careful!" said the woman. "Your IV!"

Gorku looked down at his right arm and saw that the tugging sensation he had felt was a needle hooked up to an intravenous drip. The pole the drip was connected to rattled noisily against the side of the bedframe whenever he moved his arm. He reached over to steady it, then stretched out with his other hand and snatched the sheets from the floor, pulling them up around him. His face felt hot. When he was fully covered again, he looked up at the woman, accusingly; she stared back, the corners of her mouth twitching. Her cheeks turned a soft pink. Gorku let his eyes linger on them a moment, then traced downward along the curve of her neck and over the more substantial curves below. He squirmed again, though not because of the mattress this time, and draped a concealing arm over his lap.

"You're not an old woman," he said.

"Better," she said. "Though usually when you compliment a woman it's best to talk about what she *is*."

"You have a strange accent."

"We're backsliding again. You're not some kind of desert insult comic, are you?"

"I am Azghibat Gorku, the Thundering Hooves."

"Thundering Hoofs?"

"*Hooves.*"

"Oh." She paused for a moment, unsure how to respond. "Well, Mr. Hooves, you're certainly the most interesting thing I ever came across in the desert." Her expression turned more serious. "You're lucky we found you when we did, you know. There couldn't have been an ounce of moisture left in you.

41

You looked like a cornhusk doll. Like a chronically ill mummy. Like a dozen petrified sticks of beef jerky stuck together in person-shape. Like…"

"I get it," said Gorku. "So I'm not dead, then?"

"We don't typically administer IVs to corpses."

Gorku again glanced down at the needle in his arm, as if he had forgotten it was there. He thought back over the events of the previous days, trying to process everything that had happened. All the while the woman stood there, patiently watching him. Gorku thought her face looked like a jewel, all clean, sharp lines that seemed to glitter where the light touched it. "Who are you?" he said.

"*Now* we're getting somewhere." She turned and without warning sat down on the edge of the bed. Gorku felt the soft warmth of her hips pressing against him through the sheets. His insides fluttered. Instinctively, he scooched a few inches in the opposite direction.

"My name is Francine Partridge," she said. "And if you can't tell from the name and the strange accent you so helpfully pointed out, I am an Englishwoman. Now, as for what an Englishwoman is doing joyriding through the Uzbek desert in the back of a Jeep, the answer is simple. Tell me, do you know what a *diplomatic mission* is?"

"I can't tell if you're asking me that because I sustained some sort of head injury," said Gorku, "or you think I'm a complete moron."

"Ok, fine." She held up her hands. "Far be it from me to presume what a man named *Thundering Hooves* knows about international relations."

"My name is Azghibat Gorku," he said, solemnly. "Thundering Hooves was the title bestowed upon me by the Great Horse Spirit and the members of my tribe." He then recounted the abbreviated history of the Hayal Gurununs – their exodus from the mining villages of their godless, Soviet oppressors; their elevation of Gorku as blood-heir to the throne of the great warrior-chieftains of the Khanate; their harrowing nine-day rafting expedition down the Panj; the discovery and subsequent loss of their new homeland, Hayal Gurunu; their days of wandering the riverbanks, trying to find it again, culminating in Gorku's trek into the open desert to bring back sustenance for his starving masses.

When he was finished, Francine was thoughtful. Then, after a moment, she said, "I thought we were talking about me."

"What?" said Gorku. "Oh, yes…carry on."

"Diplomatic mission," Francine repeated, and launched into a tale of a young woman, just out of university, with little direction and an overpowering wanderlust urging her to pick up stakes and follow the strumming of her heartstrings in whichever direction they vibrated.

Gorku frowned. "This is you we're talking about, right?"

Francine rolled her eyes.

Her immediate impulse had been to go to the States. In the spirit of *joie de vivre* that had overtaken her, she had vowed to pack her bags and head for the first destination that popped into her head. Like any other TV-saturated youth of the 1980s, that place turned out to be New York City. There had been just enough in her meager savings to purchase a plane ticket and two weeks lodging at a Midtown hotel. As the plane lifted off the runway at Heathrow the butterflies that spiraled through her stomach were a signal that something new was beginning. She smiled, as if pleasantly drunk. When the plane reached cruising altitude and leveled off, she pressed the button for the stewardess, asked for a bag of peanuts and was given them. Life, she reflected, was beginning to make sense.

New York City in the late 1980s was a bit more exotic than Francine had appreciated. The filth had yet to be swept from in and around Times Square. On leaving her hotel she found herself unable to walk more than a block in any direction without passing a marquee promising some combination of mammals (people, usually, but not exclusively), inanimate objects, and bodily orifices availing themselves of one another in the most distressing of ways. This was not the Broadway she had glimpsed in the pages of *Playbill*.

Nevertheless, she weathered it all with typical English stoicism and spent her days wandering the more hospitable quarters of the city taking in the sights. She had her picture taken on top of the Empire State Building and in front of the Chrysler Building. She rode a ferry to the Statue of Liberty and took the subway to Grand Central Station. She bought a pepperoni slice from a Little Italy pizzeria that cost twice as much and tasted half as good as the pizza she usually ate in London, and pronounced it the best in the world. In short, she lived the tourist's life, and with two days left of her trip she found herself with little to show for it besides some tchotchkes and a few dozen rolls of film to be developed.

Where was the enlightenment she had craved? The metaphysical divining rod she had begged the universe to unsheathe to point her in the direction of a more fulfilling life? The only arrow she had encountered on her trip was attached to her bank balance, and it possessed a distressingly earthward trajectory. "Get a job", appeared to be the message it was sending. Not terribly original, the universe, but its lessons were time-tested.

There was nothing for it but to enjoy the last few days of her trip and then board a plane back to England. Tourists were not authorized to work in the States, and Francine was too naïve and inexperienced to know any of the hundreds of loopholes around that technicality. Still, she spent the majority of her next-to-last day in New York in a coffee shop, guzzling cappuccinos and browsing the classified ads in the local dailies. It wasn't that she had expected to achieve anything practical by this; it was just a bit of playacting to prolong the fantasy she had been clinging to from the moment she had decided to leave England. But nestled within it was a real hope – too embarrassing to admit, even to herself – that somehow a miracle would occur that would set everything right and prevent her from having to slink back home a defeated woman. It was a lot to ask from the *New York Post*, but any port in a storm.

There seemed to be an unquenchable need in the States at that time for people to do "data entry", exceeded perhaps only by the dearth of "administrative assistants", bland titles that managed at once to be both specific and vague. Francine could envision a thousand permutations of each job, not one of which she could imagine herself doing for more than a week before going mad. Then there were the maid jobs and the restaurant jobs, the delivery jobs and the receptionist jobs, not to mention the less savory types of work buried in the back pages of the less-reputable rags that she was thankfully not in a position to have to consider. The ads began to blur together after a time, and so it felt especially fortuitous when her attention was grabbed by an otherwise nondescript listing in the *Times*.

She had been saving the *Times* for last, imagining it as a repository for glamorous career opportunities of the type worked by characters in the movies she had grown up watching. Oddly enough, however, the ad she was drawn to had more in common with the workaday listings she had encountered in the other papers. "Seeking Household Assistant" was the headline – to Francine it suggested a charmless fusion of "housekeeper" and "administrative assistant", while implying the worst aspects of each. Nevertheless, it would end up changing her life.

"What made you decide to answer it?" said Gorku.

"In the description, instead of *household assistant* it said *au pair*," said Francine. "Isn't that pathetic? I know they mean the same thing, but when I pictured telling my mum and my friends back home it just sounded better in my head. But the real reason was the travel – *Professional family seeking au pair to manage household. Frequent travel required, including extended periods living abroad.* Once I saw that I went straight to a payphone outside and called the number. That's the first time I ever spoke to Ben."

"Ben?"

"Ben Sanford," said Francine. "My boss. The current Chief of Mission for the U.S. delegation to Uzbekistan."

Gorku whistled. "You work for the Americans?"

Francine nodded. "Don't ask me how it happened. I called the number in the ad, Ben picked up the phone, and I just started rambling. On and on about who I was and how I'd come to the States and how I was going to have to leave soon and what a great job I would do if he just gave me a chance…" She laughed. "Honestly, I don't know exactly what I said. He told me to slow down, asked me my name

47

again. I told him, and he asked me where I was. 'Why that's only a couple blocks from here,' he said, and he gave me his address and told me to come over for a proper interview.

"I couldn't believe it. I thought au pairs needed to have a list of references a mile long. I figured he'd probably laugh me out of his house within the first minute, but I certainly wasn't going to pass up the opportunity. What was the worst that could happen, I reasoned? I hung up, walked uptown for a bit, then over to this beautiful brownstone on the Upper East Side. You couldn't look at it and *not* know you were dealing with someone important. It felt like I was trespassing just looking at it from the sidewalk. I practically had to drag myself up the steps to ring the doorbell.

"Anyway, he asked me in and we chatted for a bit. He seemed more interested in me as a person than about my prior experience. All the questions were about my life, my family back in England, my aspirations. I think he fancied me, to be completely honest. Within ten minutes he was already talking as if the job were mine."

She was silent a moment, as if replaying the video of that day in her head. "I also met his wife, Rebecca…" She curled her lips. "A cold fish, that one. She has this way of looking at you, as if you're the worst thing that's happened to her that day. When Ben introduced us, I thought my chances were shot. But after a few short questions, she just looked at me with that icy glare, then turned to Ben and said, 'She seems fine', and left the room. That was that. He offered me the job, fixed up my immigration status, and the rest is history. I've been with them ever since."

"I see," said Gorku. "And do you tell that entire story every time someone asks you your name?"

Francine turned pink again and let her head drop, an embarrassed grin on her face. "Only the ones whose lives I save," she said. "I figure they owe me."

Gorku found, for the first time in as long as he could remember, that he was also grinning. He began inching back in the direction of her hips.

"Let's try this again," she said. "My name is Francine. I'm here in the middle of nowhere with a delegation from the State Department. They're here to talk to the Uzbeks about building a pipeline or something. I don't pay much attention, because I'm just here to clean and babysit. In the evenings, during my off-hours, I take rides through the desert with one of the guys from Diplomatic Security. A couple nights ago, I came across a bearded slob sprawled out on a rock that reminded me a lot of the bums I used to see around Times Square. Against my better judgment I brought him back to camp. Better?"

"No," said Gorku. "Are you telling me I've been here for days?"

"Three nights, including the one when I found you. You've been asleep for most of it. Once in a while you'd wake up and mumble something, but that's about it."

"I've got to get out of here." Gorku swung his legs over the side of the bed and began to get up before remembering he was still naked. He retreated beneath the sheets. "My clothes," he said.

"Sorry, no," said Francine.

"Excuse me?" said Gorku.

"You're not going anywhere."

"What do you mean…?" He gawked at her, incredulous. "Give me my clothes this instant!"

Francine shook her head. "No way."

"Just where do you get…!" Summoning the cold command of his forebearers, Gorku sat up as rigid as a marble statue, shoulders thrown back, and barked, "I demand you present me with my clothes immediately!"

"You're in no condition to be up and about, let alone marching into the desert again," Francine tutted.

"So, I'm a prisoner, is that it?"

"You're a sick man in hospital," she said, taking his shoulders and guiding him down until he was lying flat. "You need rest." Gorku thought to resist, but realized with some dismay that he couldn't; he was as weak as a newborn baby. Gently, Francine took the edge of the sheet and pulled it up to tuck him in.

"What do the Americans intend to do with me?" said Gorku.

"That depends," said Francine. "Do you have any money?"

Gorku shook his head.

"Do you have any important connections?"

He shook his head again.

"Then most likely they'll wait until you're better and toss you back out into the desert."

"I don't suppose I could get some food to go. My tribe is counting on me to bring something back for them."

"If you bring them any of the stuff we've been eating, they'll probably depose you," she said. "But I'll see what I can do." A playful grin flashed across her face. "Thundering Hooves...is that really what they call you? Your people?"

Gorku nodded. "Also, Son of the Sands and The Unbending Reed. Although that last one came from the time I wouldn't let Mazar the Reckless steer our raft, and I refuse to recognize it."

Francine blinked and leaned closer, a curious expression on her face, as if she was just noticing him for the first time. "You must be the strangest human being I've ever come across."

"You're still young," said Gorku. "Give it time." He could feel the heat from her flesh wafting through her shirt, making him feverish.

"Not so young as I was." She shifted on the mattress in an effort to get comfortable and ended up draped on her side across Gorku's stomach. He drank in her shape, wasp-waisted, long and curvaceously slender. The desert sun had added a touch of bronze to her pale skin. "Time passes, and all I do is sit here waiting. Where's my great cause?" She yawned and stretched an arm toward the ceiling, the tops of her breasts bobbing to the surface above the neckline of her shirt. Gorku emitted a noise between a moan and a squeak.

"You get to travel the world," he said. "That's something."

"Maybe," she shrugged. "When you get right down to it, I'm just a glorified babysitter. Before the Sanfords' daughter was born I was just a glorified personal assistant."

"I'll let all the regular babysitters and personal assistants know the air up there isn't so sweet after all."

Francine snorted. "You're rather charming for a barbarian king, you know that?"

"I've only been at it a few weeks now," said Gorku. "Before that I was just a humble bauxite miner."

"It almost sounds like a fairy tale." She lunged forward suddenly and pressed her lips against Gorku's. He had been on the verge of coughing right as she had made her move, his throat still parched from the desert and irritated from all the talking they had done. He struggled now to hold it in, wanting to prolong the moment as long as he could.

As revered leader of the Hayal Gurununs, Gorku was no stranger to the affections of women, but he had never before experienced a kiss like this one. They were a desert people after all, and the arid climate played havoc with the lips. Kissing the average Hayal Gurunun was like smooching a belt sander. But Francine's lips were soft and pillowy. Gorku mashed his own lips against them, reveling in the greasy slickness of her lip gloss as it smeared across his face.

He was just being introduced to the joys of another's tongue being thrust into his mouth – such practices being unknown amongst his people – when the cough he had been damming up burst forth like a tidal wave. Gorku pulled his head away and started hacking like a Turkish Angora on bath day, while Francine reared back to give him space.

A moment later the tent flap opened. A woman with a pinched face slipped inside. She eyed them suspiciously. "Everything ok?" she said.

"The nurse," Francine said to Gorku, before turning to address her. "He just woke up a little while ago. He's still weak, but he seems ok."

"Thank you for that expert opinion," said the nurse, coming to stand beside the bed. "Now, if you'll excuse us…"

Gorku recovered from his coughing fit just in time to see Francine roll her eyes and smile at him on her way out of the tent. The nurse began asking him a series of questions, intermittently jotting something down on a form attached to a clipboard she held in her hand.

"We're going to need to run a few tests and then keep you a little longer for observation, ok?" she said. Gorku nodded. *Take all the time you need,* he thought. Suddenly, he wasn't in such a hurry to go anywhere.

****

Gorku remained at the camp for another ten days. It was on the second night after regaining consciousness that he and Francine made love for the first time. She had slipped into his tent after the nurse had finished her evening wellness check. Gorku had been drifting off to sleep when he heard the rustle of canvas. A shapely shadow loomed up out of the darkness at him. It crouched down at his bedside, and a pair of lips he remembered well from the previous day caressed his ear. "I wanted to wait until you'd had a chance to bathe," she whispered. Her breath felt hot and damp against his skin.

"That's nice of you," Gorku squeaked, going fully erect. Franny pulled the sheet aside and clambered up to straddle him.

They made love several times that first night, though perhaps "made love" was not the right term for it. It was clear to Gorku that Francine had a surplus of youthful exuberance saved up, and she seemed bound and determined to cash it in all at once. She writhed about, arms flailing above her head like a Pentecostal channeling the Holy Spirit, twisting her hips as if trying to wrench the cap off a pop-top bottle. It was quite unlike anything he had experienced before. *This must be that "Western decadence" Moscow always used to warn us about*, he thought excitedly.

There was no time to cuddle afterwards. The threat of discovery loomed ever-present over their trysts. A wet, sticky embrace, a quick peck on the lips, and then she was gone, slipping out of the tent with the merest suggestion of sound, like a soft breeze. In truth, Gorku welcomed these interludes. He was an injured man after all, and Francine's enthusiasms had set back his recovery significantly. The nurse couldn't understand it. "There's additional bruising here on the pelvis and stretching up along the lateral torso. You also seem to have pulled several muscles that looked just fine when you got here." She scratched her head, told Gorku both to rest and exercise more, and chalked it up to the "mysteriousness of the East". All told, Francine's visits added more than a week onto Gorku's stay at the camp, but whatever impatience he may have felt was forgotten the moment he heard the rustling of canvas cutting through the darkness each night as he lay in bed.

That impatience returned during the daytime, however, which was when he and Francine did most of their talking. She continued to visit him, as she had on that first day – in plain view, during her off hours – and they took turns expanding on their original conversation, recounting the details of their childhoods and the minutiae of their day-to-day lives, so different that it felt like they would never run out of things to say.

It had felt that way to Gorku, at least at first. It was Francine who finally pointed out how much he had begun repeating himself, returning more and more to the subject of his followers waiting for him along the Panj and the new nation he would found. Gorku apologized, but Francine would hear none of it. "I think it's incredible what you're doing," she said. "You need to leave, I understand. In fact, I've been thinking…maybe I can come with you."

"Uh…" said Gorku. It was a possibility he had never thought to consider. From the moment he had met Francine he had been dreading and steeling himself for the time when he would have to say goodbye, but the eventuality of their parting had never seemed to be in doubt. He should be elated, he realized, but something bothered him. He wondered if this was how a gameshow contestant felt who had won a new car or speedboat – sounds great on the surface, but what about taxes? What about dockage fees? Not that either of those things applied to Francine. Or did they? There was so much he didn't understand about the English.

"What about your job?" he said, at last.

"I'll quit," she said. "People quit jobs all the time."

"And then what?"

"Well, I'll be with you," she shrugged. "Become your *Chieftainess*, or whatever you call it."

Gorku was still hesitant. Francine told him to take his time and think about it, then spent the next several nights screwing every last doubt out of his system. "Maybe deep down I'm just a romantic," he said, giving her a quick spoon after his latest spinal adjustment. "I want you to come with me. I want you to stay with me, forever. Let's leave here, tomorrow night."

Francine raised herself up on the bed and gazed down at him, still panting and red-cheeked from her exertions. "My swarthy king!" she purred. Gorku forced a smile, which thankfully held until Francine began smothering his mouth with kisses.

Gorku had never slept with a white woman before. He would have been lying if he had said that the novelty of the thing didn't excite him. The reddish-gold hair, the milky skin, the blue eyes…it was all so exotic. He could hardly blame Francine for feeling the same about him. A part of him even enjoyed it. You couldn't roleplay "the marauding Hun and the Slavic milkmaid" with a girl like Francine and not gain a certain appreciation for cultural stereotypes. Still, when not in the heat of the moment there was something about all the talk of "barbarians" and "savages", delivered in a lilting English accent, that sent a chill down his spine. His head swam with images of *memsahibs* swilling gin and writing of their "shiftless, lying domestics" to their friends back home.

Lust conquered all, however, and Gorku packaged these worries into a very small box and filed them away beneath a thousand images of Francine's naked body. It was time to leave. Francine's proposal could not have been timed better. The nurse who had been treating Gorku had recently begun hinting that his recovery was complete and that he would be discharged any day; however, there were a few formalities that needed to be taken care of first. Francine learned from her driver friend that a pair of Diplomatic Security Investigators had been dispatched from the embassy in Ankara and were on their way to Uzbekistan to question him. Wandering onto the site of a proposed pipeline of vital interest to the U.S. government, it turned out, was a great way to draw attention to oneself. Gorku was not worried about the Americans. It wouldn't take them long to realize he had no interest in strategic gas reserves. But the Uzbeks were another story. He had no permission to be in the country, and chances were the Uzbek government would not look kindly on an outsider sizing up their territory for possible annexation.

When the evening of their departure arrived, Gorku waited until the nurse had completed her evening checkup, then let an additional hour lapse, when all but a small portion of the camp's security detail would have retired for the night. With the deliberateness of a cat stalking its prey, he slid out of bed, crouched down, and felt along the bottom of the tent wall with his fingertips. Eventually he came to the spot where Francine had removed one of the stakes. The canvas gave way when he pulled upward and provided him with just enough of an opening to lie down and roll through.

Gorku's tent was situated along the edge of camp, the back facing open desert. Lifting himself off the ground, he stared out across the sand rolling its way toward a horizon shrouded in darkness. Somewhere on the other side of that darkness was his tribe, waiting for their leader to return and shepherd them to Hayal Gurunu, their new homeland. Had they all managed to survive? What would they say when he reappeared? Only then did it begin to sink in just how long he had been away. He felt like Moses, returning to his flock after forty days in the desert. Although Moses had had his entire flock with him when he was wandering the desert. And he had spent forty years there, not forty days. And Gorku had only been gone for about three weeks. And had spent most of that time lying in bed and having clandestine sex with an English nanny. Still, the parallels were obvious.

There was little activity in the camp. The stillness of the night and the shifting winds played games with the few sounds that still emanated, muffling or amplifying them seemingly at random. Gorku took his time, picking his way around the camp's periphery until he located the motor pool. One of the trucks was parked away from the others, further from the center of camp and almost completely shrouded in shadow, just as Francine had promised it would be. He made a wide arc and approached it from the desert side, making the final approach on his hands and knees.

The driver's-side door was unlocked. Gorku pulled the latch and eased the door open, wincing at the moan of the hinges as it swung outward. Like a snake, he slithered up into the seat and reached for the ignition, his fingers closing over the keys that dangled there.

"Hey," hissed a voice from behind him.

Several things happened over the next two seconds. First, Gorku seemed to levitate out of his seat, smacking the top of his head on the ceiling of the truck's cabin. As he made impact, he wondered at the physical processes that had allowed him to rise more than a foot in the air without having pushed off with either his arms or legs. Simultaneously, he felt a moment of gratitude that he had neglected to drink his evening glass of water, having no backup set of robes into which he might change. And finally, as he returned earthward, his hands came to rest directly on the center of the steering wheel, activating the horn and emitting an ear-splitting "honk" that could be heard not only by everyone in the camp but most likely their bosses back in D.C. as well.

"What the hell did you do that for?!" said Francine.

"Me?" said Gorku. "What are you doing skulking around back there?"

"I told you I'd be waiting for you in the truck!"

"I didn't know you'd be hiding!"

"That's typically how one avoids being seen!"

"You didn't have to hiss like that," said Gorku. "Why not shout 'Boo!' while you're at it?"

As the couple argued, the camp gradually began coming to life. Lanterns went on in tents, flaps were thrown back, and people emerged to mill about, stretch their arms, and ask their fellow millers things like, "What was that?" and "Do you know what's going on?" A few went so far as to crane their necks. Meanwhile, the argument grew more heated.

"What would you prefer I had done?" said Francine. "Reach a hand out and grab you by the arm? Sit up and stare at you in the rearview mirror until you noticed me watching you?"

"Those are all bad ideas!" said Gorku.

"I rest my case, then."

None of those milling about seemed to know any more about what was going on than their neighbors did. Neither had the neck-craners gathered any useful intelligence. One even got a nasty crick for his trouble. A couple people began to talk seriously about moving in the direction of the noise.

"Why hissing, though?" said Gorku.

"I didn't *hiss*," said Francine.

"You did!"

"What delivery style would you have preferred?"

Gorku shrugged. "I don't know…trilled?"

"Trilled?" said Francine. "Like a bird?"

"Tinkled?"

"*Tinkled?!*"

"You know, like tiny bells," said Gorku. "Like a light, clear ringing sort of sound."

"I'm not a bloody wind chime, you clod!"

More of the millers were beginning to sign on to the idea of going toward the noise. Milling wasn't getting them anywhere. If they stopped milling and started moving they would become *investigators*, which sounded a lot cooler. They would have set off immediately if not for the guy with the crick in his neck, who was massaging it vigorously in hopes it would loosen up. The group decided to give him two minutes, after which they would leave whether he was able to accompany them or not.

"Look," said Gorku. "All I'm saying is that I got spooked. I didn't mean to press the horn. It was an accident."

Francine took a deep breath, then nodded contritely. "I know…"

"You have such a beautiful voice. I guess when I heard hissing my brain didn't connect it with you. I'm sorry."

"Really?" She twirled a finger through her hair. "You think my voice is beautiful?"

Gorku nodded.

"Trilling and…*tinkling*…" – Francine made a retching face – "…those are higher-pitched. I always thought of my voice as more…throaty." She spoke as if exhaling a plume of smoke. "Rich and smooth."

Gorku leaned toward her glistening lips. "Like a fine burgundy."

"Like velvet," purred Francine.

"Like satin," said Gorku.

"Like silk."

"Like any one of several fabrics…"

With every neck and back crick now ironed out and a consensus having been formed, the group of millers turned investigators shuffled off in the direction of the honk. Little seemed to be amiss as they approached the motor pool. They arrived to find two columns of vehicles parked beneath a canopy, and one other vehicle – a tan pickup – a short way away. The tan pickup appeared to be trembling, as if a miniature earthquake were upsetting the few square feet of land on which it sat. The investigators moved closer and leaned forward to peer inside, but their view was obstructed by the tinted windows, a darker shade than would be allowed on the streets of any town or city within the borders of the United States, but which the State Department had requested for "psyops reasons". They stood there regarding it for some moments, then turned to look at one another.

"What do you suppose it is?" asked one of them.

"It's a truck," said another.

"I know it's a truck, you imbecile! I mean what's making it move like that?"

The second man furrowed his brow as he considered the question. He was bald except for a narrow band of black hair that ran along the sides of his head and puffed out at the back, so that it looked as if he had put a sun visor on backwards. "Maybe there's a problem with the engine," he said.

"The engine isn't running," said the first man. He was tall and lean, yet oblong-shaped, his wavy hair parted severely to one side, as if someone had hung a flag atop an oversized zucchini.

"Do you hear that?" said a woman just behind them. She had the squinty eyes and flat nose of a mole that had suffered a head-on collision. "It sounds like slurping."

"Or squishing," said a third man, fingering his chin. The rest of the group started; they hadn't noticed him standing there. He had the rectangular build of a graphing calculator, and roughly the same charisma. "Also, a thumping."

"Yes!" said Mole Woman. "A slurp-thump."

"More like a thump-squish," said Graphing Calculator. Mole Woman shot him a dirty look.

"That's *got* to be the engine," said Backwards Visor.

"The engine isn't running, you ninny!" said Zucchini Flag. "Look, someone just needs to go over there, open the door, and look inside."

The rest of the group nodded and looked at him expectantly. A sinking feeling accompanied the realization that he had been elected their unofficial leader. He quickly tried to delegate his way out of the corner into which he'd backed himself. "You there," he said, searching through those assembled and settling on a stooped, gray-haired woman from Admin Services who looked like the word "grandmother" anthropomorphized. She smiled at him sweetly.

"Um…" said Zucchini Flag. "Sorry, how about you?" The group parted to reveal another man, rather average-looking in most respects yet with something slightly off about him, as if he were his own self-portrait painted from memory. "Would you mind taking a quick peek in that truck over there and seeing what exactly is going on?"

Self-Portrait shrugged and ambled over, hands in pockets, to stand beside the truck. Tentatively, he reached out, grasped the latch on the passenger's-side door and tested it. "It's locked," he said over his shoulder. The rest of the group shrugged. Self-Portrait turned back to the truck. He could hear the same "slurp-thump" (or "thump-squish" – personally, he thought it sounded more like a "squelch-ba-bump") coming from the vehicle's interior. Leaning down, he put his face an inch from the window and tried to see inside, but the tint was so dense it was like looking into a black hole. Pressing his face to the glass, he raised a fist and rapped it against the truck's roof.

A piercing cry erupted from inside the cabin, as if a sparrow were being knifed to death in the back seat. Self-Portrait grabbed his ears and stumbled backwards, toppling over onto the sand.

"Jesus Christ," said Backwards Visor, "there's a bird in there!"

A moment later the truck's engine roared to life and the tires began spinning, kicking up a cloud of sand that blanketed the faces of the investigators. Amid much coughing and gagging the truck gained traction and rocketed off into the desert with its headlamps doused, melting into the darkness.

"See, I knew you could trill," said Gorku, as he manned the steering wheel. Francine lay slumped in the back, eyes wide and chest heaving like a chain smoker who'd just taken the stairs to the top of the Empire State Building.

The truck had been pointed south, and so that was the direction they drove at first, wanting only to get as far away from the camp as quickly as possible. Once they had put some distance behind them and Francine had recovered her wits, they swung in a wide arc toward the west, knowing that at some point they would have to run into the Panj River.

"May as well put the headlights on," said Francine. "Anyone who wants to follow us will have no trouble as it is." She gestured out the back window at the two deep ruts the truck left in its wake, snaking all the way back to the camp like a trail of breadcrumbs. Gorku complied, and the landscape outside lit up in spectacular white halogen. He steered them away from the rock formations to the north and avoided the high dunes as he pressed the accelerator to the floor. The truck growled and whined like an exhausted pack animal being given the switch.

Having only made the trip by foot before, Gorku was amazed at how quickly they covered the distance to the river. In little more than an hour the ground beneath them changed, first to rock and then to the lush alluvial soils of the floodplain. As they pulled to a stop on the banks of the Panj's sluggish waters, Gorku remarked that he did not recognize any of the landmarks visible within range of the truck's high beams. This was perhaps not such a surprise for a man who had managed to lose his own country only minutes after discovering it, but if Francine entertained such thoughts she kept them to herself.

"We must be well south of where you left your tribe," she said. "If we follow the river north, we should run into them eventually."

They could not drive along the riverbank. The floodplains were too marshy to take something as heavy as the truck over them, and between them were rock formations with severe cliffs pressing right up against the water's edge. They would have had to backtrack and circle around the rocks to the sand, in which case their tire tracks would once again have given away their position. They decided to walk instead. Francine removed the supplies she had stashed in the back seat, and they abandoned the truck where it sat, hoping that whoever found it would assume they had taken to the water and headed downriver.

The trek was arduous. In order to remain hidden they stuck as close as they could to the river's edge, picking their way up and across the westward faces of jagged hills that protruded from its banks like a shark's teeth. The darkness provided them with cover but slowed their progress. Many times they found their way blocked by a boulder or crevasse that proved impassible, forcing them to turn back and reroute. Nevertheless, Gorku found the going much easier than his previous journey. Fortified by three weeks of rest and nourishment he felt as if he could walk forever, and Francine's supplies were there to answer any craving that came upon them. Even the frigid night air felt refreshing as they dragged themselves up and down the procession of slopes.

They walked straight through the night, pausing only for water breaks and to relieve themselves. As the sun poked its crown above the horizon, they increased their pace, braced by the warming air and anxious to find a suitable spot to bed down before the heat of midday arrived. The landscape had grown flatter throughout their journey. As welcome as this had been to their weary legs, Francine was worried about being seen. "Maybe we should head back to the last bit of high ground and pitch our tent up there," she said. "It's too easy for someone to stumble across us down here."

"Something about this place looks familiar," said Gorku, as he surveyed their surroundings. "Yes, over there, the opposite bank. That was where we docked our rafts after we overshot Hayal Gurunu. I'm sure of it."

Before Francine could bring him back to the matter of where to take shelter, a voice in the distance called out, "Azghibat Gorku!" Gorku looked upriver toward its source and could just make out the figure of a man in dull gray robes waving his arms above his head. Gorku half-raised an arm in response and the man jumped for joy, tripping and stumbling over his own feet in his haste to come meet them.

"Are you sure this is safe?" said Francine, but Gorku just shook his head and brushed away the question. As the man came closer, Gorku could see that it was Yelmaz the Disorganized. He threw himself to the ground at Gorku's feet, clasping his hands in front of him like a Mexican *abuela* before a statue of the Virgin. "Azghibat Gorku!" he cried. "Son of the Sands! The Thundering Hooves! Master of the Four Winds!"

Gorku raised his eyebrows – that last one was new. He cast a surreptitious glance at Francine to see whether she was impressed. "Arise, good Yelmaz," he said, in a stentorian voice. "How finds you this day?"

"Oh, brother," muttered Francine.

"I lost my wallet," said Yelmaz, clambering to his feet. "But I'm overjoyed, now that I know you're alive!" His smile faltered. "Forgive me, Great One, but there are those among us who believe you could not possibly have survived so long in the desert."

"I most likely wouldn't have if not for this young woman," said Gorku, gesturing to Francine. "Yelmaz, I would like you to meet Francine…uh, Francine…Partridge. She doesn't have any honorifics, to be honest. We'll have to work on that after we're wed."

"Master Gorku is to be married?" said Yelmaz.

"Yes, Francine has agreed to become my wife and will rule over Hayal Gurunu by my side."

A mix of emotions played over Yelmaz's face as he took Francine's hand and bowed. His eyes fairly goggled at the sight of her – all those curves where he was used to seeing only sharp angles amongst the women of the tribe. But beneath the respectful veneer and the lasciviousness, Gorku thought he detected hints of unease. He studied the man carefully, trying to put a finger on just what it was that had been bothering him.

"Yelmaz," he said at last, "what is that on your feet?"

"Hmm?" Yelmaz looked down at his feet as if only now discovering he possessed them. "Ah, the great Azghibat Gorku refers to my tennis shoes."

"Tennis shoes?"

Yelmaz nodded. "Not made for walking on sand, I know. I was in the middle of a doubles match when it suddenly occurred to me that my wallet was missing. You know how it is, when a realization like that pops into your head out of nowhere. Anyway, I ran right off to look for it. Didn't even occur to me to change my shoes." He scrunched up his face. "Say, you haven't noticed any wallets lying around out here, have you?"

"Uh, no," said Gorku. "Did you say *doubles match*?" He looked Yelmaz up and down. "I say, you're looking rather fit these days."

70

Yelmaz blushed. "It is kind for the great Azghibat Gorku to have noticed."

"You don't have to keep calling me that," said Gorku. "Tell me, how have the people faired in my absence. Has everyone survived?"

"Oh, yes!" said Yelmaz. "In fact, something rather miraculous took place not long after you wandered into the desert. A man appeared, who...well, maybe it's easier if I just show you. Come, bring your Blessed Consort!" He beckoned for them to follow as he tromped off, his lost wallet forgotten once more.

Franny turned to Gorku, a look of pleasant surprise on her face. "I didn't know your tribe had a tennis court!"

Gorku frowned. "Neither did I," he said, stalking off after Yelmaz with a sense of foreboding.

****

It was a very long swimming pool. That is how Gorku would have described it, having few points of reference for such things. In fact, it was roughly twice as long as the average football pitch is wide, minus about a third. Were it filled with nickels rather than water it would contain enough money to purchase a mint-condition 1986 Ferrari Testarossa, as well as many, many other things.

Gorku and Francine stood on the edge of the pool looking down at the man sprawled on top of a giant, inflatable cactus. The floating man grinned up at them despite the patchwork of sunburns covering his body, so intensely red they seemed to vibrate. In his hand was a whimsical glass filled with some sort of fruity cocktail.

"I'm sorry," said Gorku, "just once more from the top. You're who, now?"

"Radislav Zulitsky," said the floating man, flashing a set of thousand-watt teeth. "And no need to apologize. I'll tell you whatever you want to know. Any man reluctant to talk about himself must not love himself. And loving oneself is the necessary first step to building a better world."

"Says who?" said Gorku.

"That's one of my own." Zulitsky laid a hand across his chest. "I call it a *Zulitsky-ism*."

Gorku frowned. "Look, why did you bring my people here? What is this place?" He gestured at the rows of thatch-roofed bungalows, palm trees, and beach umbrellas surrounding the pool, as if a Sandals resort had spontaneously burst from the ground and started offering all-inclusive deals.

"You're looking at the nerve center of Zulitsky Enterprises," said Zulitsky. "Our new corporate headquarters."

"Headquarters?" said Gorku. "That's what this is supposed to be?"

"Actually, we like to refer to it as a *Thinksphere*," said Zulitsky. "But you'll learn all about that during your orientation."

Gorku started to speak but was distracted by an incessant thumping noise. A short way from where he stood a large, open-air building with a tropical-chic décor emitted a steady stream of electronic dance music.

"That's Oasis, our five-star bistro and cocktail lounge," said Zulitsky, following Gorku's gaze. "Go ahead, grab a drink. It will change your life. The bartender is a certified *rummelier.*"

"I'll pass." Gorku looked on with dismay as a moment later Francine slipped away and made a beeline for the bar. "What kind of company is this, exactly?

"We like to say that our mission is to unlock the latent potential of the human spirit."

"Well, that certainly sounds like it's on the up and up. Must be why your home office is in the middle of the Central Asian desert."

Zulitsky shrugged and cleared his throat. "Certain tax and legal realities made it advantageous to relocate our headquarters in a more eastwardly direction."

"I'll bet." Gorku paused to shield his face as Beghnir the Brave went hurtling past him to do a cannonball. "Nice one!" said Zulitsky, steadying his drink as his cactus bobbed up and down on the resulting waves.

"Look," said Gorku, "you still haven't explained what my tribe is doing here on your…headquarters."

"Not tribe," said Zulitsky, shaking his head. "Countrymen!"

"What do you mean?"

"It just so happens that Zulitsky Enterprises sits perfectly within the bounds the sovereign nation of Hayal Gurunu, whose existence was declared only a few short weeks ago. It's a tiny nation, but prosperous. Zero percent unemployment since its inception – what other nation-state can boast that?!"

Gorku tried to respond but found that he was speechless. His jaw sagged as if a tailor had been instructed to take it out a few inches. "I…I don't understand," he managed at last. "Is this a business or a country?"

"Exactly!" Zulitsky threw up his hands. "That's what's so beautiful about the whole thing. Whether we pay a corporate tax rate of zero or a hundred percent it doesn't matter, the money ends up in the same place. Our citizens all work for the State, yet we're a completely capitalist society. Our regulators and our executives are the same people. Talk about creating efficiencies!"

"But…Hayal Gurunu is supposed to be our homeland!" said Gorku.

"And it is! Under the aegis of Zulitsky Enterprises. Not only did your people gain a homeland, but also job security, room and board, and amenities comparable to some of the finest resorts in the Mediterranean."

"We already had job security, we had room and board," Gorku sputtered. "What we wanted was freedom!"

"You've got it," said Zulitsky. "Everyone is free to leave whenever they want. Go ahead, ask around. See if anyone tells you they're being kept here against their will."

Gorku thought about calling his bluff, but a quick look around showed nothing but smiling faces. Beghnir the Brave splashed around the shallow end of the pool like a little kid. Elgbar the Shameless lay stretched out on a deck chair, completely nude, soaking up the sun. Across the courtyard, in a leafy grotto, Pashtina the Equivocator indulged in a half-hearted yoga routine. They all looked healthier and happier than Gorku could remember ever seeing them. Gritting his teeth, he turned back to Zulitsky.

"What exactly is this company of yours?" he said. "What have you got my people doing?"

Zulitsky launched into a long-winded explanation of the Zulitsky Method. Gorku listened, not sure if he was following everything. Hugs were important, he gathered. The universe was a circle, and hugs formed a circle. There was a lot of talk about paradigms, both old and new. Ions factored into it a great deal, especially positive ions.

"Yes, but what is the actual product you're selling?" said Gorku.

"The Zulitsky Method Starter Pack provides customers with all the tools they need to achieve self-actualization using the body's natural gravitational pull. Once an individual has located the authentic self, there's no limit to the practical uses to which the Zulitsky Method can be put. We sell courses on tax preparation, psychoanalysis, home edecorating, you name it!"

"But are they books, or...?"

"Oh, yes," said Zulitsky. "And CD-ROMs."

"You're telling me that my tribe is hawking self-help courses over the phone to gullible Westerners?"

Zulitsky's cactus seemed to deflate a little. "It sounds sort of cheap when you put it like that." He took a long pull from his cocktail, then suddenly brightened again. "But that's exactly why I need you as my Vice President for Strategic Marketing."

"Your what now?" said Gorku.

"You're absolutely right," said Zulitsky. "We've been thinking too small, making cold calls all day. We need to reach the people where they are. Television spots. Seminars all across the U.S. and Europe. An annual conference in Vegas for our biggest earners."

"I didn't suggest any of those things," said Gorku.

"And yet your presence alone brought the ideas to the surface," said Zulitsky. "We at Zulitsky Enterprises have a term for people like you – Creative Catalysts. You bring out the best in those around you. It's no wonder your people look up to you so much."

All of a sudden, Zulitsky sat up straight on his cactus and grasped his head as if he were having a migraine. The glass with the remainder of his drink slipped from his hand and fell into the pool. "I've just had another brainstorm! What if we enlisted our most successful customers to help pitch the product? For a modest, upfront fee we could provide them with their own starter and add-on packs that they could independently sell, reupping their supply whenever it runs out. Then they, in turn, could recruit some of *their* best customers to become independent sellers and purchase product from *them...*"

"You mean a pyramid scheme?" said Gorku.

"Legally, no." Zulitsky stroked his upper lip. "There's a distinction, I believe. I'll have the lawyers check into it." At a look from Gorku, he raised his hands. "Admittedly, there would be a triangular aspect to the flow of revenue being generated. But that's just the nature of business, isn't it?"

"I wouldn't know," said Gorku. "We didn't grow up with such principles. And frankly, I have no desire to be introduced to them now."

"Look," said Zulitsky, "we're talking about executive-level compensation here. You'd be pulling in a six-figure salary to start, *plus* a five-percent share of the company. If this thing keeps growing the way I think it will you'll be a millionaire in just a couple years. And you know what? You're worth every penny. These people here hold you in great respect."

Gorku nodded. "They do. And I refuse to betray that respect for your filthy lucre."

"My what?"

"Your filthy lucre!"

Gorku stomped away before Zulitsky could respond, rounding the pool to where Beghnir was busy doing underwater handstands. He waited for Beghnir to surface, then told him to get out of the pool and follow along.

"Where are we going?" said Beghnir.

"To Hayal Gurunu," said Gorku.

"But we're here, Great One."

"Not this…Devil's waterpark." Gorku grimaced. "I mean the true Hayal Gurunu. Our homeland, that's out there somewhere waiting for us."

Beghnir followed Gorku's gesture past the edge of Zulitsky's property to the open desert beyond. As if on cue a swirling wind kicked up a cloud of sand that spun and lashed about like a tornado made of angry hornets. Its ghostly howl could just be heard beneath the thumping of the dance music coming from the bar.

Beghnir clenched his teeth. "Out there?"

Gorku nodded.

"I'll pass."

"What?"

"I think I'm going to stay here for a bit. Maybe later," he added conciliatorily, "just…not right now."

Gorku's mouth hung open. From the corner of his eye, he could see Zulitsky watching from his cactus perch, a smug expression on his face.

Leaving Beghnir, Gorku went next to Elgbar and then Pashtina to try to make his case, with similar results. Soon he found himself running through the compound, entreating anyone he could find to abandon the false paradise they inhabited and follow him into the desert. The response was uniformly negative. They had been tired for so long, they told him. Hungry. Thirsty. Bored stiff. There was swimming here. And air conditioning. An all-you-can-eat shrimp buffet from three to five. Eating shrimp in the desert is gross, Gorku pointed out. Conceded, they said, but it beat the heck out of eating nothing.

Gorku was checkmated. There was nothing for it. He tried one last entreaty to his followers' patriotism, but without a nation of his own to offer them his words rang hollow. Summoning his remaining dignity, he thrust back his shoulders, spun smartly on his heels (had he been wearing a cape, he would have twirled it) and marched off toward the exit.

On his way out he stopped to grab Francine. He found her bellied up to the bar, surrounded by a trio of empty rum glasses and two gentlemen dressed in brightly colored ponchos and wide-brimmed sombreros that formed something of a canopy over her head.

"I'm leaving," said Gorku.

"Darling," Francine slurred, as if he hadn't spoken, "I'd like you to meet a couple friends of mine, Rick and Joe."

She gestured to the two men hovering behind them, watching their conversation with what Gorku found to be an unsettling intensity. "Hey," he said, nodding. They tipped their hats in response.

"Rick and Joe were just telling me about the Zulitsky Method," said Francine. "It's really quite fascinating!"

Gorku frowned. "It's a scam, Francine. A bunch of New Age mumbo-jumbo."

"Not exactly," one of the men interjected. Gorku couldn't tell the two of them apart. Along with the costumes they wore, their faces and hair were nearly identical. Gorku decided to call the one who had spoken 'Rick'.

"Don't listen to these...*salespeople*." Gorku spat out the word 'salespeople' as if it were a piece of food with a hair on it. "That's their job, to make stupid things sound interesting so you'll buy them."

"Not salespeople," said Rick. "We are outsiders here, just like you. We arrived only a couple of days ago, with the intention of discussing some of the finer points of this 'Method' Mr. Zulitsky has been proselytizing."

"Oh yeah?" said Gorku. "Did he enlighten you?"

"Quite the contrary," said Joe. "After some preliminary discussion it became clear to us that Mr. Zulitsky is, as you say, a sort of flimflam man."

"At least we agree on something," said Gorku.

"Did you know Jesus used the power of hugs to invent quick-dry concrete?" said Francine.

"Um…" said Gorku.

"Rick and Joe told me." She paused to take a swig from a fourth drink that had somehow materialized in her hand. "He started out as a carpenter, just like everyone thinks. But then during his missing years in Galilee he was visited by beings from another planet. They taught him to embrace his fellow man, and that all living creatures, great and small, are God's children." She put a hand to her mouth to cover a belch that had snuck up on her. "I guess he took it literally, because right after that he started wandering the countryside preaching about love and hugging everyone he saw. He also started telling everyone that he was the son of God."

"We probably should have been clearer that we were being metaphorical," said Joe. Rick's eyes went wide, and he jabbed an elbow into Joe's ribs.

Francine continued. "Anyway, after a few years of this, all those hugs must have unlocked some sort of cosmic portal in his mind. One night he had a dream where he saw the formula for quick-dry concrete written on a stone tablet. He woke up the next morning and vowed to use his newfound knowledge to build low-cost housing for the poor. Unfortunately, Rome's marble and granite guilds caught wind of the plan and got spooked. They thought he would start undercutting them for the big temple and coliseum jobs. They made a few calls back to the capital, and next thing you know he was up on a cross."

"That's a hell of a story," said Gorku. He shot a glance at Rick and Joe. "I suppose I should thank you both for keeping my fiancée entertained in my absence."

"You are welcome, of course," said Rick. "Though our intention was not to entertain, but to warn."

"Warn about what?" said Gorku.

"Zulitsky," said Joe. "I fear he is playing with forces he does not fully understand."

"I wouldn't worry," said Gorku. "Quick-dry concrete's pretty common these days."

"There are mysteries far greater than concrete," said Rick, ominously.

"Listen," said Gorku, turning back to Francine, "you don't have to come with me. You can stay here if you want, or go back with the Sanfords."

Francine had been mulling over that very question, right up until the time Rick and Joe had introduced themselves and interrupted her train of thought. It was the reason she had run off to the bar to begin with. According to the training her handlers had given her she should have been on her way already, back to the Americans with some sort of cover story ready. Gorku had no power base left; his followers had abandoned him. As a potential asset he was worthless. And yet…

It wasn't that the story she had given Gorku was untrue. The stuff about coming to the United States on a whim, about answering an ad for an au pair job and getting hired by a top diplomat, had all happened. It's just that there were a few key details she had omitted. Like how the ad had been brought to her attention by a friendly, well-dressed man at the coffeeshop who also happened to be from England.

How the friendly Englishman, unbeknownst to Francine at the time, had an associate of his make some calls and fax over a doctored resume to the Sanford residence ahead of her visit. How the Englishman knew that Ben Sanford had a thing for college-aged girls and frequently cheated on his wife. How, not long after she had been given the job, she had run into the Englishman while taking a stroll through Central Park, where he had revealed that he was with MI6 and had filled her in on the other side of the bargain, the things that were now expected of her.

Gorku had been a side project. She almost hadn't bothered mentioning him in her weekly report to her handler, so she was surprised when the instruction came back to develop a relationship with him. "It's the Wild West over there right now," her handler had said. "Anyone with any pull could be useful to have on our side. If this guy's got a hundred-odd people trailing him through the desert, he must have some kind of influence."

Only they had all gone over to Zulitsky now. She should probably report back to her handler about him. He seemed like the kind of guy who would have some dirt they could leverage – tax fraud, shady business practices, something. But all she could think about was Gorku, this strange man who never felt at home where he was and so decided to pull up stakes and create a home of his own, a place where he could feel truly free. She realized she admired him. Maybe even loved him.

"I'm not leaving you," she said. "Not ever."

A smile crept across Gorku's face. As thunderstruck as he felt from all that had happened, her words still warmed his heart. He hoped it wasn't just the alcohol talking.

Gathering their supplies, Gorku and Francine said goodbye to Rick and Joe, then left the bar and headed toward the desert. As they neared the exit, Gorku could hear Zulitsky's voice behind him, addressing the group. "What you have witnessed here today, ladies and gentlemen, was a prime example of the emotional-spiritual black hole I've been warning you about. A once great leader picked bare by the vulture's beak of negative thinking. Let his weakness act as a warning!" It was all Gorku could do to keep himself from running back and dunking Zulitsky's head underwater to go look for his missing cocktail glass.

They walked for a mile or so, just far enough that Zulitsky Enterprises (Gorku would never think of it as "Hayal Gurunu") could no longer be seen. The midday sun made it too dangerous to go further, even if Francine had not surrendered a good portion of her motor skills to Zulitsky's daiquiris. On the far side of an outcropping that provided them with some shade, they set up their tent and crawled inside to wait out the remainder of the day. Even Gorku, upset as he was, sighed contentedly at the coolness that washed over them.

They lay on their backs, feeling the uneven sand pressing against them through the floor of the tent. Gorku stared upwards, hands behind his head, while Francine fidgeted and pawed at him tentatively, unsure what she should say or do under the circumstances. "It's going to be ok," seemed the safest choice, to which Gorku just grunted. Even to her own ears the words sounded empty, not to mention a bit garbled and boozy.

There were certain other things, however, that she was still proficient at, even with a few drinks in her. She leaned in close and ran her tongue along the curve of his ear, then down along his neck, covering him with sloppy kisses. After a few moments he began to respond, and she rolled over to mount him, ducking her head to avoid hitting it on the roof of the tent. They both came quickly, then fell apart, more tired than before but still unsatisfied, restless. Francine tumbled heavily back onto her spot. She wanted to tell him one more time that she would never leave him, to reaffirm her love for him, but it wasn't a moment after her head hit the wadded-up dress she'd arranged as a pillow that she fell into a deep and dreamless slumber.

When she awoke again it was dark inside the tent. Francine propped herself up and ran her tongue around the gauzy insides of her mouth, too groggy to notice or wonder at how much time had elapsed. She felt around for her bag and dug out a bottle of water, taking a long swig, then reached over to see if Gorku was awake and offer him some. Her hand came up empty. She put the bottle down and felt around some more, then got up onto her hands and knees and crawled over to Gorku's side of the tent. He was not there. The clothes he had been using as a pillow were missing, along with the bag of supplies she had packed for him. The only thing her hand brushed against was a piece of paper, folded in half, which she was unable to read no matter how closely she brought it to her face.

Francine's heart began to pound. Even as she scrambled from the tent and peered out into the desert, she knew she would not find him. The full moon overhead rendered the landscape an impressionistic painting of shadow and silver-blue light; only the rock outcrop and the area immediately around her stood out in any detail. Not a footprint could be seen except for her own leading back to the tent. It was as if the entire world had shrunk down to a few hundred square feet. She felt suddenly very small and alone, retreating a few steps even as she yearned to run forward and search every dune until she found him again.

She had almost forgotten the note in her hand, until the sound of rustling paper in the breeze shook her from her thoughts. Picking out a spot away from the rocks where the moonlight was brightest, she unfolded it and began to read:

Dearest Franny-

As I lay here considering our situation, the one truth that keeps asserting itself no matter how much I try to deny it is that there exists but a short window during which your life can still be salvaged. Unfortunately, every additional second you spend in my company closes that window a little more. I have nothing to offer you – no homeland, no tribe, no future. Go back to the camp, to your old life. Tell them whatever you have to in order to save yourself. Say that I kidnapped you. Say that I was a religious fanatic who hoped to ransom you. It no longer matters because I won't be around to suffer the consequences. Believe me when I tell you that these last few weeks have been the happiest of my life, and that it is only the profound love I feel for you that allows me to walk away now, knowing that it is the best gift I could possibly give you.

Until we meet again on the plains of Uçmag…
                              Your swarthy barbarian king

Francine spent the rest of the night curled up on the floor of her tent, eyes brimming with tears, cursing Gorku's name and vowing with all her heart to defy him. But by the time the sky began to brighten, the impertinence had drained out of her. She lay there like a child in the aftermath of a tantrum, recognizing the futility of doing anything other than what he had asked her to do.

Gorku was dead. She could feel it in her bones. Were she to wander into the desert after him she too would be dead within a week, no matter how many supplies she brought with her. Once these truths had sunk in, she felt a sudden desperation to be off. Filling her bag with whatever water was left, she abandoned the tent and struck out into the still-cool morning, heading for the banks of the Panj.

Only a mile away was Zulitsky's compound. She could make a call there, ask someone for a ride back to camp. But nothing in the world could ever make her set foot there again. Instead, upon reaching the Panj, she began backtracking downriver toward the spot where she and Gorku had left their truck the night before last. No longer worried about being spotted, she avoided the high ground and stuck to the flatter terrain further in toward the desert. This made the going much quicker, so that the heat of the day had barely begun by the time she spotted the truck in the distance. It was exactly where they had left it, only now there were two other trucks parked nearby. Leaning against them were a pair of security officers, talking to one another with arms crossed, looking bored out of their minds.

Francine paused for a moment out of their line of sight, bracing herself for the lie she would have to start living from the moment she revealed herself. She said a silent goodbye to Gorku, letting the tears well up once more, before leaving her hiding spot to half-run, half-stagger toward the officers, waving her arms and shouting for help.

They were startled at first, drawing their firearms, but by the time she had reached them they recognized her and were helping her into the back of one of the trucks, as she babbled incoherently about being held prisoner. Eventually she allowed the officers to calm her and sat in silence while they radioed to camp to inform the higher-ups that she had been located. No one spoke on the drive back. Francine did all she could to discourage questions, staring out the window in a sort of catatonic state. There would be plenty of time for explaining herself later, she knew.

****

Xyghitix Florp and Kleinmerp Bazzlewind stood in the lobby of the Silk Road Motel Bar & Lounge waiting to be checked out. The proprietor, an elderly gentleman in a traditional *chapan* and *tubeteika*, ran down the list of incidentals.

"I'll have to charge you for the extra towels," he said.

"We understand," said Florp. "We got a little carried away, I'm afraid."

The proprietor waved a hand. "No need to explain. I know how Ryballians are with towels."

Florp shook his head. "I still can't believe you recognized us."

"Please," said the proprietor. "You think you're the first Ryballians who ever stayed here?"

"Well, yeah, kind of," said Florp.

"We get all kinds," said the proprietor. "You should see how Neptunians treat the bedsheets."

While Florp remained waiting at the desk, Bazzlewind paced about for a bit before taking a seat on a nearby bench. On the wall opposite, in a gilded Victorian frame, hung a painting showing a street scene from a medieval European city. Along one side of the painting a group of townspeople ran rampant through a row of market stalls, looting and pillaging, while in the foreground dead bodies lay strewn about the road, having succumbed to some sort of plague. Further along, on the other side of a wall sconce, was a smaller painting depicting a domestic scene from a Dutch household several centuries ago. A brooding father in ruff and breeches sat at his kitchen table, staring gloomily down at his shoes. His wife, in peasant garb, stood across from him, forlornly pouring the contents of a pitcher into a bowl. Between them, on the floor, three children cavorted wildly, mouths frozen in mid-shriek; one of the children reached out to yank the tail of a spaniel, who stared out of the painting with a resigned expression.

"I don't understand art," said Bazzlewind.

"What is to understand?" said the proprietor. "It is enough to feel. Art dramatizes and lends nobility to the suffering of the world."

"Is there a lot of suffering here?"

"Quite a lot! It is the human condition to suffer."

"On our planet, whenever we see a problem we fix it," said Florp. "Now everyone is happy."

"But friends," said the proprietor, "think of all that you are missing. The rich emotional tapestry that you will never get to experience."

The Ryballians were silent. "I think I understand," said Florp, after a moment. "Just as we have no mosquitos on our planet, we are denied the pleasures of bug spray." He nodded. "Yes, I can see how this is regrettable. You have given us much to think about, Earth human."

They settled the bill, then thanked the proprietor and bade him goodbye, dragging their suitcases outside into the bustling streets of Tashkent. A taxi picked them up and took them across town, stopping along the way so they could make a few last-minute purchases, before finally depositing them on the outskirts of the city. Standing by the side of the highway they looked like a pair of hitchhikers. Rather than stick out their thumbs, they gathered up their belongings and lugged them away from the road, out into the desert. Their ship was not far away, concealed beneath a camouflaged tarp on the back side of a dune.

When they had reached the ship and uncovered it, Florp hopped into the driver's seat and started the engine, turning on the air-conditioner to let the cabin cool off. Then he got back out and circled around to the cargo hold to help Bazzlewind load their bags. On top of their suitcases they placed the new possessions they had bought on the drive over – an insectarium packed with *aedes aegypti* and a couple crates of Raid. The time had come, they realized, to start living life to the fullest.

The Birth of Ennui

The joy had begun to fade. Around the back of the birthday boy's chair the family stood arrayed in a loose horseshoe, arms pressed tightly against their sides or draped across their neighbors' shoulders, tentatively, as if something damp and unpleasant resided there. Across from them, at the other end of the dining room table, stood the boy's mother, wielding a camera at them much as a bank robber might wave a pistol at a row of petrified tellers. She peered through the viewfinder, sizing up the scene before her, which hid for a moment her severe, disapproving expression.

"Left!" she said, in a whip-crack voice. Gloomily, the horseshoe complied, scuttling leftward en masse like some enormous, drunken crab. Grumbles and recriminations issued from its component parts as cousins, uncles, grandparents, and other more distant relations – some who had clearly imbibed several glasses past their limits – stumbled over one another.

"Too far!" said Agatha, for that was the boy's mother's name. The horseshoe snapped to attention. Its two-dozen eyes blinked perplexedly as it awaited orders. It didn't do to anger Agatha, even when she was badly outnumbered. An enormous, drunken crab they might have been, but they understood the concept of self-preservation.

"Constance, quit scrunching so!" Agatha's younger sister flinched at being addressed directly and attempted to decompress herself, like a crumpled ball of paper newly released from a squeezing hand. She rolled her shoulders back and stood in an approximation of straightness, arms held several inches out at her sides, as if in each hand she held an invisible shopping bag. Yet no matter how she contorted her limbs she seemed to occupy only a fraction of the physical space allotted to someone her size. The remaining void, those who knew her well would tell you, was her missing self-esteem. She was, as always, at the far end of the horseshoe.

Agatha exhaled, an ill-omened hiss like the seal breaking on a vampire's sarcophagus. "Cuthbert, *really*!" she said. No more was needed. For Agatha, the word "really" was a sentence, if not paragraph unto itself. Uncle Cuthbert allowed the Danish that was perched upon his bottom lip to slip from his fingers, trembling at the brittle *clink* it made as it plunked face down on the plate below. The plate he placed gently on the table as his eyes darted to and fro, more to avoid his sister's gaze than to ascertain who else might be watching him.

No one was watching him, it turned out, as all attention was focused on the center-front of the horseshoe, where the boy's cousins were having a row. Tiny hands fluttered about in the space between their faces while bony elbows prodded the stomachs and hips of their elder relations. They were each as slight as their father, Cuthbert, and mother, Prudence

94

– who stood just behind her sons, looking upon them with an expression of amused exasperation – were fat, as if two capital *O's* had given birth to a pair of lowercase *l's*. Prudence raised her eyebrows and said in a lilting voice, "Jeph, Potty...remember your Ephesians!"

Behind the camera Agatha rolled her eyes. Her sister-in-law was a born-again Christian, a fact Agatha could tolerate so long as it had the decency to stay bottled up within the four walls of Prudence and Cuthbert's home. Unfortunately, Prudence was rather loud and proud about the whole thing, to the point where she had chosen the Old Testament names "Jephthah" and "Potophar" for her sons. Expecting the rest of the family to wrap their mouths around such abominable monikers was a bridge too far (even Prudence had to admit the "ph-th" in Jephthah left her tongue-tied), and so the children became known popularly as "Jeph" and "Potty".

"Head full of wool, that sister of mine!" steamed Agatha. "What's wrong with Mark and John? Aren't they in the Bible? And rather major players, what?"

Thomas, Agatha's husband, shrugged. "Some people enjoy being obscure."

Thomas was notably absent from the horseshoe just now. The boy's father had run to the supermarket to get ice cream. "*Vanilla* ice cream," hissed Agatha, as Thomas went out the door. There was plenty of ice cream in the house, several gallons in fact, including such fanciful varieties as Fudge

95

Twister, Double Chocolate Brownie, and Cherry Potter. (Being a sucker for puns, this last one had caused Thomas to titter like a schoolgirl in the middle of the frozen snacks aisle upon its discovery.) On returning home with his bounty, his reception had been somewhat more subdued than he had imagined it would be. "Dolt" and "simpleton" had been bandied about with alacrity. Couldn't he, inquired Agatha, carry out even the simple task of obtaining a sugary treat without mucking the whole business up? Before the door slammed shut behind him, he heard Agatha add, "And regular vanilla, none of that French business!"

Ephesians having made less an impression than Prudence had hoped, the cousins were now locked in a sort of death grip. Jeph grabbed a tuft of Potty's hair as if it were a clump of stubborn weeds he was trying to uproot, while Potty pinched Jeph's ear between thumb and index finger, twisting it like a housekey in a particularly stubborn lock. They yowled and hissed at one another like a pair of tomcats.

"Leggo, you plank!" screamed Jeph.

"Piss off!" said Potty. "Let go of my hair first!"

"You nonce!" Jeph attempted to bring his other arm around to ensnare Potty in a headlock, but another twist of the ear made him squall. "You fight like a girl!"

"Who's the one pulling hair?" said Potty. He thrust about wildly with his free hand, trying to land

96

what passed for a punch on his brother's unguarded stomach. "You perv! You sniff women's underwear!"

"You *wear* women's underwear!"

"You sniff *boy's* underwear!"

Agatha thought it important, even after all these years, to give her sister the time and space in life to do the right thing; only after Prudence had demonstrated once again that she was incapable of doing so did Agatha step in to clean up her mess. Where family pictures were concerned, she had less patience than usual. It required the most coordination of any activity her family engaged in and unfailingly laid bare their foundational flaws, like a shoddily built tract house that fell to pieces at the first stiff wind. Abandoning any thoughts that this year's photo might go off without a hitch, she set the camera on the table, placed her fingers to her mouth and began to blow. The ear-splitting whistle that emanated from her brought an immediate halt to all pushing and grabbing, grumbling and muttering. A heavy silence descended on the room. No one dared move a muscle. It was as if the party were a television recording that had been put on pause.

"*If* we might," said Agatha. A moment's hesitation, then all throughout the horseshoe individuals began resituating themselves – brushing out wrinkles from their clothes, fixing hair, digging through purses for lipstick or blush in order to apply a last-minute touchup. An involuntary détente achieved, Jeph and Potty released one another and straightened their sport coats. A malaise settled over the group, as if they were a class of misbehaving schoolchildren whose principal had just arrived to put an end to their fun.

Cowed now and more or less arranged, the family stared gloomily at Agatha. Never one to tempt fate, she snatched up the camera and began snapping wildly, right at the moment Thomas stepped in through the front door. He peered at them over the top of the paper sack he was holding. "Are we doing the picture, then?" He looked around for a place to put the shopping bag, but it was too late. The shutter ceased its clicking and the horseshoe began to dissolve, each guest drifting off to find a spot where they could hunker down and begin concocting a reasonable-sounding excuse to leave early. Most of the men gravitated toward the living room, where the TV was blaring; the women tended toward the kitchen for a chat; while Jeph and Potty marched grimly toward the basement stairs, intent on bringing their armistice to a swift and violent end. Thomas kicked off his shoes and jostled past them, bag still in hand, and made his way over to Agatha. "I'm not in the picture!"

"And?" she said, her voice like a snapping turtle. "Neither am I. What's done is done. We know what we look like."

Thomas looked around in distress at the rapidly emptying dining room. "But...but I've missed 'Happy Birthday'. I've missed the cake!"

A slight shudder, barely perceptible, passed through Agatha. She glanced over at the table to find the boy still seated there, staring down disconsolately at the spot where his cake presumably should have appeared. In her haste to rid herself of that most distasteful of tasks, the family photo, she had forgotten that several other, only slightly less distasteful tasks remained. There was nothing for it – she would have to wrangle everyone back into the dining room.

"Thomas," she said, "bring them back to the dining room."

"Who?" said Thomas.

"What do you mean who? All of them!"

"Ah...yes dear." Thomas put down the grocery bag and went about the business of imploring the guests – most of whom wanted nothing more at that point than a stiff drink and a soft couch to rest upon – to return. As he shuffled off to the living room, he heard behind him a rustling of paper followed by a disgusted groan.

"Ice milk?!" said Agatha.

Thomas paused on the threshold of the living room and turned, sheepishly, to face her. "It was the only vanilla they had."

Agatha nodded and glared at him, a tight-lipped smile creasing her face, as if deriving a grim satisfaction from the fact that every shortcoming she'd ever charged her husband with possessing was eventually borne out. The carton she clutched in her hand perspired beads of condensation, which gathered into rivulets that trickled down the length of her forearm. Rather than put the carton down or reach for a napkin to dry herself, she maintained her posture and added the unpleasant sensation to the debit side of Thomas's ledger.

"*Gather*...the guests," she said.

It was a decidedly less cheerful horseshoe that reassembled itself around the dining room table and aimed its chorus of frowns at the birthday boy, before whom Agatha had placed a cake. It was a round, store-bought number, white-iced with a swirling green-and-blue floral pattern around the border and the words, "Happy Birthday, Fergus!" piped in teal in the center. For indeed, that was the boy's name, young Ferguson Thrush – Fergus, for short – who was this day turning eleven years old, as evidenced by the eleven tiny candles Agatha jabbed into the cake as if sticking pins in the voodoo doll of a hated enemy.

Once the candles had been lit and the room lights dimmed, Agatha took her place at Fergus's side, looming over his shoulder. "Everybody?" she said. She hummed a few bars in D minor, then counted off, "Three...two...one..." The guests began to sing, in dirge-like tones:

> *Hap-py birth-day to you,*
> *Hap-py birth-day to you,*
> *Hap-py birth-day dear Fer-gus,*
> *Hap-py birth-day to you.*

"Now make a wish," said Agatha, but Fergus had already blown out the candles, his wish being to end the party as soon as possible. There was a smattering of applause from those assembled, which quickly waned and then died out altogether when one of the candles that appeared to have been extinguished regained its flame.

Agatha feigned a polite chuckle. "Fergus," she said, and gestured for the boy to finish the job, but try as he might he could not put the candle out. What began as a dispirited effort grew more determined and then turned frantic as the tiny flame refused to yield, withstanding the gale-force winds Fergus unleashed upon it with increasing frequency. Each time the wick, seemingly reduced to a smoldering ember, reignited, Fergus would gulp an ever-larger mouthful of air – cheeks swelling like Dizzy Gillespie – lean forward and unleash it upon the candle like a twister descending upon some Midwestern telephone pole. Aware of the embarrassed looks the guests directed at him and each other, he began to huff and puff without pause, a steady stream of air in and out, in and out, like the chugging of a steam engine. Sweat glistened across his brow and his complexion turned first a fiery red, then pallid, the blood draining from his body. The guests' embarrassment soon turned to curiosity, then concern.

"He's hyperventilating!" said Cuthbert.

"For God's sake, do something!" cried Prudence, wondering if she had just taken the Lord's name in vain. She crossed herself, just in case.

Thomas stepped forward and placed a hand on the boy's shoulder, entreating him to stop, but Fergus gave no indication he had heard his father and continued to blow. Soon Agatha stepped forward and joined Thomas in grabbing the boy by each arm, attempting to drag him away from the table. Fergus resisted at first, but eventually lack of oxygen and the realization that he was beaten worked to calm him. He looked about in a daze as he was helped into the living room and laid down upon the couch to recover.

"Get those blasted candles out of here," Agatha whispered to Thomas, once their son was situated. Thomas nodded and hurried off, happy to have a task he could carry out to his wife's satisfaction.

"Now, now then," said Agatha to Fergus, who sat staring off into the middle distance. "Now, now."

"He's tired, is all," said Cuthbert, unhelpfully.

"He's not tired," said a stentorian voice. It came from the Thrushes' next-door neighbor, Graham Stockings. He peered down at Fergus over the top of a rocks glass, his dark, pomaded hair reflecting the light from the ceiling lamp above to form a halo. He twisted his mouth, which only further accentuated his chiseled features. "He's *thinking* about something." At the sound of his voice,

Constance's cheeks flushed red and she scrunched herself back up into a ball.

"I'm just not good at anything," said Fergus, unhappily.

"Well, who is?!" said Agatha. "Look around you. Do you see a surplus of talent in this room? Your father can't even buy ice cream correctly!"

Thomas, who had disposed of the candles and was about to inquire as to who wanted dessert, quietly slunk from the room.

"Uncle Bromley can write," said Fergus.

"So can some great apes," said Agatha. "It's hardly elite company. And stop calling him *Uncle* Bromley. He's Prudence's brother."

"And proud as punch about it!" came a genial voice from the perimeter of the group, where Bromley Waxpole had been biding his time. He elbowed his way to the front now, clutching a slim book whose cover he subtly maneuvered so that all assembled had a chance to glimpse it. "Proud to be a part of this family, to share in moments like…"

"You are *not* a part of this family," said Agatha. "Prudence insists on your coming to these gatherings, and Cuthbert gives in to whatever foul scheme his wife concocts. And, as Cuthbert is my brother and I am not without a certain sense of propriety, a chain reaction is created which results in your being here – every…single…time."

Waxpole stood grinning with the dumb good-naturedness of a golden retriever. His head – curiously oval-shaped and topped with tight, brown curls – protruded from the neck hole of a ribbed sweater that struggled to contain his ample girth. Taken as a whole, he resembled nothing so much as a bowling pin atop which a Brillo pad had been affixed.

Agatha regarded him coolly. "I suppose you want to read a passage from your book now, is that it?" Bromley raised his eyebrows expectantly. "Oh, go ahead," said Agatha. "The boy seems impressed by your scribblings. Maybe you'll cheer him up. Or put him to sleep. Either way, problem solved."

Waxpole registered the insult, but being as shameless as the next writer he chose to ignore it and dive straight into a sampling from his recently published memoir, *Just One More Hour: Life at 5AM*, which concerned his travails working the early shift at a local café, and his desire for more sleep. It was his third such memoir in as many years, following his debut, *Life Before Sunrise: The Relatable Lament of a Working Man* and last year's *As the Rooster Crows: A Caffeinated Life*. Waxpole often repeated the dictum that one should "write what they know", ignoring the fact that one needn't write at all. Like clockwork a new tome rolled off the presses each November, eliminating the need for guesswork on the part of Waxpole's Christmas gift recipients when a thin, rectangular parcel inevitably appeared beneath their trees.

Waxpole cracked the cover and thumbed past the introductory text until he found the page he wanted. "Chapter one," he intoned, "Humble

Origins." The other guests cast nervous, sidelong glances at one another, finding themselves ensnared in a literary event.

"I was born on a mink farm," Waxpole began. "Don't ask! My father was a sea captain, and my mother was a woman with a thing for sea captains. It was love at first sight..."

"Our father wasn't a sea captain!" said Prudence. "He piloted the bike ferry on the Abernathy-Boorhouse Recreational Trailway!"

Waxpole chuckled and began to squirm. "Which crossed the sea..."

"It didn't!" said Prudence. "It crossed the Ainsley River..."

"Which *empties* into the sea..."

"Five-hundred miles downriver!"

"What about the mink farm?" said Graham Stockings. "Why bring it up if you don't want people to ask about it?"

"It's called building mystique!" Waxpole huffed and snapped the book shut. "I see people are getting irritable. We'll try this again after everyone's eaten."

"Ah yes..." said Agatha. "The ice milk."

The scene quickly shifted back to the dining room, where Thomas had already cut the cake into slices and divvied it up amongst a row of plastic bowls. The guests ate heartily, not even minding the ice milk, as the escape it provided from Waxpole's dreadful prose made it taste all the sweeter. The only one not partaking in dessert was the birthday boy himself, who remained prostrate on the couch staring up at the spider-web patterns on the plaster ceiling and wondering how an eleven-year-old boy with no obvious hardships could possess the brooding temperament of a Chekhov protagonist. Such sadness without source was its own cause for distress, a vicious cycle dragging him down into a perpetual funk through which he moved every waking moment, a heavy, gauzy thing hanging off him like a wet comforter.

Perhaps, he thought, he should take up a hobby; the banality of the suggestion only depressed him further. Being good at nothing he enjoyed nothing, and the pursuit of something, anything, would serve only to compound his suffering. Was there nothing in life that required little effort, allowed no chance of failure, yet provided one with a deep sense of fulfillment? It was a question for the ages, but if any of the great philosophers had ever ruminated upon it, it was news to him. Probably too hung up on stuff like "ethics" and "metaphysics" to busy themselves with how the lazy should feel good about themselves. The Epicureans gave it a decent go, but while they were very good at identifying what a person should aim for (freedom from fear, absence of bodily pain, etc.), they didn't leave much of a roadmap for how to achieve it. More practical advice could be found in the pages of his mother's *Good Housekeeping* magazines, where articles with titles such as 'Living a Stress-Free Life' and 'Tips for Increasing Your Happiness' went right to the heart of the matter. "Take a pass on perfection," one article began. This was the sort of achievable goal Fergus could get behind.

Yet no matter how often he fixated on his imperfections, happiness remained elusive. *Maybe I really am just a 'Gloomy Gus'*, he thought. That's what Mr. Stockings, the neighbor, had remarked once when he encountered Fergus frowning on the front porch. "Hey, there's a Gloomy Gus!" he had said, coming up the front walk. It had taken Fergus some time to realize that Stockings had been talking to him. He hadn't felt particularly sad at the time, but he was certain Stockings had been referring to his ever-present frown, a feature seemingly baked into his face, encoded in his DNA. Stockings had patted him on the head then and popped inside for who knows what reason. He was always coming around, "just to see how's doing" he would announce in an annoying, faux-folksy way.

Is that why I feel so melancholy all the time, Fergus wondered? The frowning? *Good Housekeeping* said one way to increase happiness was to smile more. If that was true, Fergus reasoned, then the inverse likely was true as well. If so, the implications were dire. He could no more stop himself frowning than he could stop his heart from beating.

From the other room, the sound of Agatha's voice cut through the din. "Fergus! Come and have your dessert, love, your cake's getting soggy!"

Fergus frowned (or perhaps remained neutral, who could tell?), rolled from the couch and trudged into the dining room with the grim determination of an infantryman approaching the front at Verdun. As he crossed the threshold the others turned in unison to look at him, offering words of welcome and encouragement that rang hollow in his ears. To his credit, as self-pitying as Fergus could be, he reserved his greatest pity for those others who were forced to contend with him. He knew it could not be easy adhering to form, observing the customary social niceties with a miserable sack such as himself. His skin crawled now at being the center of attention, the forced joviality with which people addressed him, as if all their words had exclamation points stapled to the back of them.

Fergus accepted his bowl of cake, cradling it as if it contained the ashes of a beloved pet. In the corner of the room nearest the picture window, his birthday presents were stacked upon the floor – boxes of various sizes wrapped in shiny striped or polka-dotted paper that glinted in the sunlight. He ran his fingers up and down the handle of his spoon, staring down at the sugary soup in which it swam with the shattered countenance of a lovesick cowboy who'd pawned his guitar. Closing his eyes, he envisioned the scene that would shortly play out, rehearsing in his mind the words of thanks he would deliver as he unwrapped each package, a liturgy as rote as any in Christendom. At least two of the packages, he was certain, contained turtleneck sweaters. He could feel it in his bones.

Leaving Paris Behind

The ball was thrown high, high enough that the play-by-play man felt the need to comment on it, as he did every time DeMolay served. When it reached its apex it hung for a moment – inertia and gravity, in their tug of war, having reached a stalemate – a neon-yellow blemish against the faces of a thousand, tiered tennis enthusiasts who gasped their appreciation in a collective, "Ah!"

When gravity inevitably gained the upper hand, the ball began its spiraling descent, hurtling toward the man known as 'Jacque the Rock' to his most fervent supporters. Like a seasoned limbo champion, he arched his back, shoulders parallel with the ground, and held his racket out at his side; his arm, fully extended, showed sinewy muscles that rippled with anticipation. Eyes directed toward the heavens, he traced the ball's tragic fall from the airy heights of Roland Garros to the steaming clay beneath his customized K-Swiss.

And then…a crack! As though it were spring-loaded, DeMolay's body erupted into motion, a furious windmill swinging his racket high, he struck the fuzzy orb cleanly on its face and launched it with laser-like velocity at his adversary, who stood rooted in place like a traumatized weed.

"Net," said the line judge.

DeMolay watched the ball pitter-pattering at the foot of the nylon at mid-court. It was his seventh double-fault.

"You suck!" yelled someone from the upper deck.

"Quiet please," said the line judge.

DeMolay finished out the match, a crushing loss to virtual unknown Spencer Shoe, ranked 137th in the world. Even worse than the humiliation of losing to a Yank amateur on French soil was the headline that greeted him the following morning as he sat down for his customary breakfast of toast and orange juice: 'DeMolay Has Seen His Day'. To be dismissed in rhyme, he felt, was the height of ignominy.

These feelings were compounded when he received a tearful phone call from his girlfriend, Tamara. Her distress could also be traced to the newswires, this time her hometown paper, the *Pittsburgh Post-Gazette*: 'Shoe Stomps the Competition' it read, accompanied by an Op/Ed piece entitled, most bewilderingly, 'For DeMolay, the Shoe is on the Other Foot'.

"What does that mean?" asked Jacque.

"It means you're washed up," said Tamara, who, being American, had a succinct and often jarring way of delivering the truth. "You're a terrible tennis player," she added.

"I see."

"No, you don't see," she snapped. Jacque marveled at Tamara's ability to transcend grief. "If

111

you did see, you would have given up the sport long ago."

"But I love playing tennis…"

"Oh, can it! You don't love tennis. You mope every time a tournament comes along. You barely even practice anymore. You're getting old, Jacque…"

"I'm only thirty-two."

"That's old for a tennis player."

"What about the money?"

"That was fine, back when you could actually win a match. You'd probably make more now managing a grocery store."

"Well, thanks for cheering me up."

"You want cheered up? Buy yourself a Hallmark card. But don't ask me to keep excusing you for letting your life go to shit."

Jacque was racking his brain for an exceptionally biting comeback when he heard the line go dead. Tamara had an exquisite sense of timing, especially when it came to arguments. Manipulation and subjugation, he thought, those were Tamara's true talents. She would have made an excellent psychologist, or fascist dictator.

DeMolay got dressed and left his room at the Saint Germain Holiday Inn. His lodgings had been a last-minute choice, born of necessity after his coach, Bertrand, had informed him that his sole remaining sponsor, Texas-based Riggings Athletic Gear (slogan: "The Game is Rigged"), had refused to put up the funds for a two-week stay at the Hotel Bel

Ami. The Saint Germain Holiday Inn had the advantage of familiarity. It was like any other Holiday Inn anywhere in the world, albeit slightly 'Frenchified' – a few gaudy, ornamental touches on an otherwise slipshod design. This concept was perhaps best encapsulated by the lid of DeMolay's toilet, an Italian marble piece with gold inlay, which, when lifted, revealed a cracked, plastic bowl conspicuously absent of water. The latter was due to a broken pipe, which management had assured would be fixed as soon as possible – "as soon as possible", apparently, being more than seven days, which is how long DeMolay had been relegated to using the lobby restroom to relieve himself. His subsequent calls to the desk had been received with an indifference worthy of Marie Antoinette. "You've got your marble toilet lid," it seemed to say. "What the hell else do you want?"

The hallways of the Saint Germain Holiday Inn were narrow, and long to the point of absurdity, so that the walls, rather than run parallel, seemed to angle slowly toward one another, terminating at a sharp point somewhere off in the distance. This trick of perspective, coupled with the serpentine patterns of the floor carpet, set DeMolay's mind reeling, and his thoughts fell inevitably on Tamara – Tamara, at home in Pittsburgh; Tamara, driving to and from the bank; Tamara, stopping by Saint Ann's to pick up their daughter, Marguerite; Tamara, cooking dinner; Tamara, washing clothes; Tamara doing the dishes. There was something steadfastly American in the way Tamara trudged through life, never slowing down, never questioning. It was this undying conviction, and the stability it provided, that Jacque found her most admirable quality, and yet it never failed to send a chill through him when he considered it for too long.

Leaving through the Gothic double-doors (another superfluous amenity) at the front of the lobby, Jacque stepped out onto Rue Cavalier, into the heat and haze of Norman summer. He chose a direction, left, and started walking, rising and falling as the uneven concrete demanded. He passed a café on his left, a smattering of umbrella-shielded tables spread across the sidewalk where old men swirled their wine glasses and young, brooding couples frowned over their café crèmes. Farther up to his right, a string of boutiques had attracted a herd of glamorous waifs, long-limbed beauties who eyed the dresses and bags displayed in the windows with detached amusement.

Watching the leisurely pace of Saint Germain, the people drifting and bobbing like buoys in a dead sea, DeMolay realized that, after a decade spent living there, America had become a part of him too. His motherland he viewed now through a foreigner's eyes, and what he saw was movement, movement without focus, without endpoint or destination. No goal existed; it was the movement of the restless, the pacing of one stuck in an empty room. He thought about this as he passed the fountain on Rue Amèlie, the spot where, twelve years earlier, he had held a young American exchange student named Tamara Woodlawn in his arms and kissed her for the first time. How decrepit it looked now, the cracked marble covered in creeper vines and stained with mildew. The water had all but dried up. The spickets had been turned off and the bowl held only a few stagnant puddles choked with leaves. The city had not seen rain in over a month and a half. Paris was in drought.

When he had finished his walk, DeMolay packed his bags and called for a taxi to take him to the airport. He had succeeded in upgrading his ticket, snagging a seat on the redeye to New York after another passenger had cancelled last minute. His family would not be expecting him for another three days. Jacque felt the surprise might do them good. He thought of Marguerite's expression as he walked through the door, how happy she would be to see him. The name 'Marguerite' had been Tamara's idea, pretty girls' names being "one thing the French got right." Jacque realized he had forgotten to buy his daughter a present. He spent the hours before his flight was to depart searching the meager offerings of Charles de Gaulle International, settling finally on a souvenir pen and a stack of notebooks for her to write her stories in.

Marguerite, he was proud to tell people, had a certain knack for writing. She had a knack for almost everything she tried – painting, sculpting, poetry, music, sports. There was a vigor with which she attacked life, a tiny sponge trying to soak up everything at once. He wasn't sure if it was the normal exuberance of an eight-year-old or something intrinsic to her personality, but he hoped she would never lose that fire, would never stop finding joy in discovery.

The flight itself was without event, a lack of turbulence making for a serene passage, as if the plane were gliding on a surface of ice. Unable to sleep, DeMolay browsed through a magazine he had purchased at an airport newsstand. The cover had caught his eye, specifically one of the smaller headlines near the bottom-left of the page, promising analysis and dissection of 'The Ten Greatest Tennis Matches of the Nineties'. Jacques was astounded to see his photograph underneath, taken twelve years ago at the final of the NEC Open in Phoenix. Tagged by *The Sporting News* as "one to watch", the twenty-year-old DeMolay had upset Pete Sampras in a five-set marathon the press had dubbed, as befit the times, "Desert Storm II".

DeMolay read the article, a set-by-set breakdown of the entire match, and as the words touched his eyes and wormed their way into the recesses of his brain, the memories unfolded, stretched themselves out like an old, forgotten reel of film removed from its canister, so that he could almost feel the Arizona sun beating down on his neck and the blisters that tore at his feet as he navigated the baseline. Those were the days of infinite promise, the days when things came easy, when tennis and love and life had been a source of constant joy.

Which, as he arrived at the final period of the final sentence, made the return to his present reality that much harder to comprehend.

Touching down at LaGuardia just before dawn, it was then onto a Greyhound for the seven-hour drive to Pittsburgh. Jacque watched the familiar scenery roll by, fields interspersed with trees, followed by hills and the occasional farmhouse, the sort of dour landscape destined to be enshrined on the walls of a local McDonald's. He fought down a sudden craving for French fries and dozed the majority of the trip, preferring his dreams to the gray reality of Pennsylvania's skies.

It was early evening when they arrived in Pittsburgh. Sitting in the back of a Yellow Cab, winding through the East End toward his home in Point Breeze, Jacque imagined the reception he was about to receive. Marguerite would run to him, no doubt, clutching a picture or story or whatever it was she was working on in school. He would look at it, smile, and tell her how talented she was. Tamara would glance at him and immediately go back to whatever she had been doing. "I thought you weren't getting back until Wednesday," she'd say, not really expecting an answer and not caring if she got one. After that she would ignore him. He'd take her out to dinner later, perhaps a show at Heinz Hall. Bribery had long ago proven the quickest and surest way to her heart.

"Looks like it might rain," said the cabby, and indeed it was only a moment later that Jacque heard the rhythmic tapping of raindrops against the windshield, starting off slow, then growing into a steady drizzle that blanketed the city outside.

"Seems like it's always raining here," said Jacque.

The cabby shrugged. "That's Pittsburgh for you."

Jacque was somewhat dismayed, as the cab turned onto Linden Street, to find Tamara's car sitting in the driveway. There would be no time to prepare, then; no time, either to change his mind. He paid the driver and hoisted his bags from the trunk, stumbling somewhat as he climbed the narrow steps leading up to his porch. All up and down the street the front windows of the houses were lit, their quiet glow familiar and reassuring.

He paused in front of the door and looked through his own window. Tamara, he could see, was seated on the couch. In front of her, on the floor, was Marguerite. Mother was brushing daughter's hair, a second-rate Movie of the Week blaring away on the television. Jacque took a deep breath and sighed. Thirty-two years old, he thought. There were worse things. Bracing himself, he twisted the doorknob and stepped inside.

Tales of the Landed Gentry

Part I. The Duel

Here's a story that sounds invented but is true. Not that every last detail is factual right down to the letter, but the events I'm about to describe to you are not fabricated. That is to say, while the story has been assembled from various scraps of gossip, innuendo, hearsay, and rumor, its central truth cannot be disputed. And those that have disputed it have employed distortion, prevarication, disinformation, and double-speak to achieve their ends. Everything I tell you now was relayed to me, personally, by indisputably credible sources. And the sources from which my sources received their information, I was assured, were really top-notch.

So, here goes – it concerns a private tennis match between Roland T. Calhoun, the scion of a wealthy American Band-Aid manufacturer, and Sir Alistair Shrewsbottom, 5th Earl of Shrub's End. Long an admirer of the American 'can-do' spirit, it was the Earl's habit to invite men of prominence from across the pond to visit him on his sprawling estate, Cromwell House, where he lavished them with the finest food and drink from around the world. Perhaps because his was inherited wealth, bestowed rather than earned, the Earl's zealous generosity had the feeling of atonement, an apology that doubled as an assertion that he belonged in the same class as these self-made titans whom he entertained. Roland T. Calhoun, for instance – not content to live idly on the substantial allowance his father provided him – had made his own fortune by trademarking the term 'Band-Aid', then suing his father's company for infringement. It was exactly this sort of initiative and drive the Earl respected.

One area where the Earl's generosity did not extend was the tennis court. It was here, on the manicured grass surface of his private playing grounds, which he dubbed 'The Meadows', that the Earl sought to test his mettle against the world's best. To this end he spared no expense, going so far as to finance once-a-month steamship passage so that the great Hazel Hotchkiss Wightman herself could tutor him. By the time of Roland T. Calhoun's visit in 1924, it was widely agreed throughout the British Isles that no one could whack a ball like old Shrewsbottom, and aristocrat and commoner alike took a certain patriotic satisfaction in the Earl's clinical dissection of one Yankee bigwig after another.

Some background before we get to the matter at hand. Only two weeks before the match in question, the Earl had caused a minor diplomatic kerfuffle when, at a cocktail party at the American embassy in London, he had tipsily referred to the visiting Zelda Fitzgerald as a "gin-soaked floozy who married her way into respectability". The ferociousness with which the ambassador had leapt to Ms. Fitzgerald's defense confirmed the suspicions of the ambassador's wife that the two of them were having an affair. The evening came to an abrupt and noisy end, culminating in the Earl's ejection from the premises by two beefy, young Marines into the back of a waiting cab. Through the disorienting fog of a hangover, the Earl awakened the following morning to a telegram from the Prime Minister's office, informing him that he should not be expecting an invitation to any of the Crown's functions in the foreseeable future.

So, it was in a climate of strained Anglo-American relations that the motorcar carrying Roland T. Calhoun pulled up in front of Cromwell House's iron gates. Happily for the Earl, his visitor seemed blissfully unaware of his cocktail party gaffe, and even less concerned for the dignity of Zelda Fitzgerald. "I don't care much for them New York types," he said, giving the Earl a chummy slap on the back. "Maybe I'm just an old southern bumpkin, but I can't think of anything New York has that Alabama don't." The Earl could think of quite a few things, but experience had taught him the virtues of keeping his mouth shut.

Over a dinner of boiled eel and beetroot salad, the Earl unveiled for Calhoun his recent prize purchase – a custom-made, Draper & Maynard racquet with otter-skin grip and reinforced gossamer webbing.

"Well, I'll be!" said Calhoun, grateful for the opportunity to furtively dispose of his food in a nearby potted fern. "That there is a fine piece of equipment!"

The Earl, boasting of his new racquet's lightness and aerodynamic qualities, offered to let Calhoun take a few practice swings there in the dining room. The latter assented, darting this way and that, his right arm swinging wildly as if he were riding an invisible bucking bronco. So engrossed was he, "Yee-hawing!" and "Ya-hooing!" to his heart's content, that he failed to maintain proper gripping technique; after one particularly impassioned swing, the racquet came loose from his hand and propelled across the room, smashing at last into an ornate vase perched atop the mantelpiece.

"Ho!" said the Earl and rushed to inspect the damage. It was, as they say, not good. The carnage called to mind the children's rhyme *Humpty Dumpty*, but whereas Humpty Dumpty had been a man – or an egg, or an egg-shaped man, the Earl had never been quite clear on this – the shattered heap before him was of a far more valuable provenance. He calculated his chances of repairing the damage and found his spirits un-bucked. Even with "all the King's horses and all the King's men" on the job, they had still been forced to chalk Humpty up as a miss. As an Earl, Shrewsbottom had considerably less resources to call upon. His only man – that being his valet, Hives – was not exactly what you'd call "hot shakes" with a tube of glue.

"Golly," said Calhoun soberly, as he joined the Earl. "I guess I went and made a mess of it, huh?"

To his credit, he offered to pay whatever it cost to replace the broken vase, but the Earl just shook his head. If it had only been a matter of money the Earl would have laughed the whole incident off, perhaps even smashed another vase himself in a spirit of camaraderie. This vase, however, possessed sentimental value. Worse yet, the sentiments belonged to the Earl's father, retired General Horatio Herbert Shrewsbottom. Shrewsbottom *père* had brought the vase home with him from Africa after leading a regiment in the Sudan Campaign. It was his only spoil of war and a prized memento, but its lilac-and-periwinkle flower pattern was exactly what the Earl had needed to tie his dining room together, and so he had slipped it beneath the folds of his overcoat while paying his father a surprise visit the month before. He had fully intended to return the vase after Mr. Calhoun's visit, or at least that's what he had told himself. It hardly mattered now. The road to Hell was paved with such things, he reflected – good intentions, that is, not lilac-and-periwinkle vases.

"If he finds out I nicked it, I'm finished," said the Earl. "My ears will come in for a sound boxing. Have you ever had your ears boxed by a retired British general, Mr. Calhoun?"

"No, sir, I have not."

"Consider yourself among the fortunate. Generals are known to have uniformly large hands."

The prospect of an ear-boxing having ignited his adrenaline glands, the Earl was not long in concocting a plan to get out this sticky situation. As it had been his hand that had dealt the fatal blow, Roland T. Calhoun agreed to help in any way he could. So it was that two days hence, an interview with the visiting "American captain of industry" appeared in the morning edition of the *Shrub's End Daily Observer*, where, amongst a list of innocuous observations of the "British-people-drive-on-the-left,- American-people-drive-on-the-right" variety, mention was made of the declining state of the British military, which hit its nadir, according to Calhoun, "around the time of the Sudan Campaign", where it required "twenty-thousand troops with machine guns to take out a bunch of camel-riding yokels dressed in bed sheets".

That same afternoon, the Earl got in his motorcar and went to pay his father a surprise visit. He found the aged relative pacing about the drawing room in an apoplectic rage, clutching a newspaper. "Have you seen this bilge?!" he said by way of greeting, shoving the paper in the Earl's face.

"In fact, I have," said the Earl.

"What does this uncouth, Confederate bandage merchant know about war?! Someone ought to take him down a peg!"

"Coincidentally, that's why I came to see you. It just so happens that I have challenged this Mr. Calhoun to a tennis match, but The Meadows is being re-seeded and I have nowhere to host it. Would you mind very much if we used your court?"

"Mind? I insist! Call this rabble-rouser and schedule the match, forthwith. I'll have the grounds crew get everything prepared."

The Earl and Roland T. Calhoun faced off the following morning in the General's cavernous, private stadium. They were alone except for the owner himself, as well as his household staff, whom the General had excused from duties and ordered to sit in the stands to cheer his son to victory.

Unbeknownst to the elder Shrewsbottom, this dovetailed perfectly with the Earl's plan, for as the match commenced, the Earl's valet, Hives, was simultaneously tiptoeing his way into the General's house to deposit the remnants of the prized vase on the floor of a guest bedroom which overlooked the court. Having done so, he slid open the window and waved a white handkerchief, the agreed-upon signal that all was in place.

Down below, Roland T. Calhoun was receiving a right thrashing. He had of course agreed to throw the match beforehand, and he was doing a splendid job, sending forehands and backhands, lobs and drop shots alike careening around the grounds. The Earl had taken the first set 6-0 and led the second 5-0, with the serve for match point. The General was beside himself with glee. "Go on, Alistair!" he bellowed. "Send this blighter back to the States with a pair of goose eggs!"

A flash of white caught Roland T. Calhoun's eye. He looked across the court at the Earl and winked – everything was ready. The Earl tossed the ball high and sent a soft, high-bouncing serve towards Calhoun, who cocked his racquet back and gave the ball a mighty wallop, sending it soaring over the bleachers and fence surrounding the court, straight through the open window of the guest bedroom, from which there emanated a mighty crash.

"Christ, what was that?" cried the General, and went running off with his staff to investigate. When they had gone, Calhoun and the Earl met at center-court. "Well, I suppose now I owe you one," said the Earl.

"Don't mention it," said Calhoun, as a flashbulb ignited off to their side. The Earl turned, surprised, to find a photographer from the Daily Observer. "I decided to use all the controversy surrounding the match to gain a little notoriety and score an introduction with one of your big medical supply manufacturers," said Calhoun. "I'm going to sell 'em on leasing the name 'Band-Aid' from me, make myself a fortune."

"Glad I could be of assistance," said the Earl. "Might I ask which firm you're planning on meeting with?"

Roland T. Calhoun was about to answer when a pair of hands the size of frying pans appeared on either side of his head and clapped him soundly on the ears. "Hmph!" gasped Calhoun, emitting a gurgling sound not unlike the purr of a tubercular cat. He tottered off, weaving like a punch-drunk infant, as flashbulbs exploded in the background.

"Can you believe it?" said the General. "That twit's gone and broken my vase!"

Several months later, the Earl was lounging in his drawing room when Hives entered and handed him a letter. "My word, Hives," he said, after skimming it over, "this letter is from Roland T. Calhoun. You'll never guess what it says. Turns out that the pictures of my father clapping poor Role on the ears made it all the way to America. One day Role was sitting in his office when he got a telephone call. He picked up the receiver, and there on the other end was Zelda Fitzgerald! She told him she'd seen the pictures in the Times and recognized 'that horrid Limey from the embassy' – she's referring to me, there, Hives – and wanted to get in contact. Turns out our Zelda is also from Alabama. The two hit it off from the word go. They've been spending so much time together that old F. Scott is beside himself with jealousy. He's apparently taken to rewriting the novel he's been working on – *Gatsby of West Egg*, or something like that – and added a character based on Role! Ever read any F. Scott Fitzgerald, Hives?"

"Yes, sir," said Hives.

"What do you think? Anything to him?"

"His work is not without its merits, sir."

"Hmm. Seeing as how I'm somewhat responsible for all this, I guess you could say that I've influenced literary history, what?"

"One could say anything, sir."

"Precisely. I believe that's enough work for one day. Draw the curtains, Hives. I wish to rest."

Part II. A Race to the Finish

Lord Ambrose Farthing awoke feeling chuffed to the gills, not to mention the scales, the fins, and the rest of his fishier parts. It was the sort of morning that lent itself to stepping out on one's terrace, taking a long, deep breath, and sweeping one's gaze appreciatively over life's bounty. Unfortunately for Lord Farthing, his accommodations were conspicuously terrace-free, and the only bounty to be seen from his window was the heating and air-filtration system on the roof of the convenience store across the street. So elevated were our Lord's spirits, though, that he betrayed not a whit of disappointment, and in fact spent several minutes in silent appreciation of the Mini-Star News and Grocery's elaborate ductwork.

Lord Farthing opened the window and let the cool, Andorran air waft over him. True to its geographical origins, it felt equal parts Spanish and French against his cheeks. Though he had spent much time in both those countries and travelled often between them, he had never before set foot in Andorra itself, treating it more as a sovereign median strip to be avoided on jaunts between Barcelona and Saint-Tropez.

Spreading his nostrils and drawing in the aforementioned breath, Lord Farthing felt tightness in his chest and a mild burning sensation creeping up the esophagus. A thin gruel indeed. He was a good deal higher up than was typical in his native London.

Mountains, Lord Farthing felt, were best left to goats, and the Pyrenees were proving no exception. A jagged heap of granite and gneiss named for the rape victim of a Greek demigod, it seemed to him a perfectly natural metaphor for the antipathy the Spanish and French people felt for one another, a giant scar marking the place where their nations slowly ground each other into dust. God, Lord Farthing reflected, was the ultimate poet.

It was the morning of the 21st annual Andorran Grand Prix. This, Lord Farthing had been assured during a rather rummy lunch at The Terriers in London a fortnight earlier, was a car race of sorts. Lord Farthing knew little of racing, his previous exposure to the sport being limited to a chance encounter with a thing called 'NASCAR', which he had been forced to endure as the only available entertainment during a flight delay at Hartsfield-Jackson International Airport. From what he had been able to discern, NASCAR consisted of several dozen automobiles retrofitted as billboards, carrying their messages of 'Tide' detergent and 'Kenny Rogers Roasters' screaming around a gigantic oval at breakneck speeds, to the primal screams of a hundred-thousand primitive hill folk (descendants of Scotch-Irish immigrants, he later learned). That such a thing was being bandied about The Terriers as if it were a perfectly suitable conversation topic filled Lord Farthing with deep misgivings for the future of Britain.

Grand Prix, though, was not nearly as bad as all that, according to his company. Europe had worked hard to put its special gloss on the production, and the results were sleeker cars, a more sophisticated audience and more beautiful race tracks – "circuits", as the Formula One crowd called them. Farthing seemed to recall a big to-do about a Grand Prix when he last visited Monaco, but nothing short of nuclear war or an empty drink glass could have diverted his attention from the baccarat table that weekend. As the charming waitresses of the Casino de Monte Carlo had kept him up to his nose in gin fizzes, such an event had not been in the offing.

Any sort of race not involving a dog or horse was normally *thema non grata* around 'The Big Table' (as Lord Farthing and his circle referred to their usual place setting in The Terriers' dining room). On this occasion, however, Buppy Turlington-Brown ("Lord Turlington-Brown", he called himself, though his claim rested on a great-uncle who was a baronet, or something equally ridiculous) had invested heavily in an Italian driver with the unlikely moniker, Sergio Letargo. Not a name to inspire confidence, but then Buppy had never lacked for the stuff. Now that he'd tossed a few million pounds into the mix, suddenly he was an expert on all things automotive. Lengthy dissertations on the positioning of exhaust exits and the legal usage of flexible rear wings gave way to flights of poesy regarding "hairpin turns 'neath the dense conifers of Hockenheimring".

If weathering Buppy's presence were a chore on the best of days, dealing with the man as he dissected the minutiae of the Hamilton-Massa collision at Singapore required Sisyphean levels of patience. Lord Farthing fell decidedly short of that mark, and one evening – as Buppy interrupted a rather ribald analysis of the relative virtues possessed by the contestants in that year's Miss English Diamonds pageant to hold forth on vented nosecones – he excused himself from the table and hurried home to book the very next flight to Andorra.

What fueled this sudden excursion was, put simply, spite. Knowing that all the "harrumphs" and "ahems" in the world would not be enough to give Buppy the hint, the only option remaining to Lord Farthing was to acquire a driver of his own, beat the pants off Sergio Letargo, and shut up Lord T-B once and for all.

Andorra, as it happened, was where the next scheduled Grand Prix was to be held. This would be Lord Farthing's scouting trip. He was prepared to spend, and spend big, having pawned several pieces from his art collection at a recent Sotheby's auction, including Rubens' *Caesar Taking a Shvitz* and Van Dyck's *Portrait of a Weimaraner*. It was with the straightened spine and dignified bearing of one who had just received a monumental infusion of cash that Lord Farthing stepped off the plane at La Seu d'Urgell and was taxied by helicopter to Andorra la Vella.

The Andorran Grand Prix, Lord Farthing had been informed by his concierge upon arrival at the Sport Hotel Hermitage, was the crown jewel of Andorran society, every bit as central to its identity as cigarette smuggling and trying to convince outsiders that Andorra is a real country. "We've a Prime Minister and everything," said the concierge. Lord Farthing patted the man's head and handed him a euro.

Back to the morning at hand. Having taken his breath and contemplated the ductwork, Lord Farthing went downstairs to commandeer a taxi to take him to the Grandvalira Circuit, where the Grand Prix was to be held.

"Going to the race?" said the cabbie, a little too familiar for Lord Farthing's tastes. "You'll love it. It's the most important in the world. All the best bikers will be there."

Lord Farthing felt certain he had misunderstood his chauffeur, or that "biker" was some obscure Andorran colloquialism he was not familiar with. On being deposited at the entrance to the aforementioned Circuit, however, he was dismayed to behold several dozen men in brightly colored, polyester bodysuits and goggled helmets astride motorcycles, revving their engines in anticipation of the starting signal.

The Grand Prix of Andorra, it turned out, was a 'Supermoto' event, according to the woman at the ticket window, a ghastly sounding hybrid of "on-road motorcycling" and "motocross". Lord Farthing extricated himself before the woman could explain the difference, certain that this knowledge could only affect him for the worse. He had assumed the term 'Grand Prix' referred exclusively to a Formula One car race, but translated literally, of course, it meant only 'Big Prize', something that Farthing – even with his low marks – should have remembered from his primary school French lessons.

A wasted trip then, but Lord Farthing vowed to make the best of it. A young, single lord with several million newly acquired pounds in the coffers who can't make a go of it in a European tax haven was hardly worthy of his title. Andorra had no casinos beyond the odd hotel slot parlor. What it did have was shops – shops everywhere, of every conceivable shape and size, selling every conceivable good. Find a building that was not a shop and there was a good chance it was a bank. Wherever one looked, money was moving, an endless cycle of withdrawals, expenditures and deposits that formed a sort of vortex, sucking in any wealthy sophisticates that passed too near its horizon. Lord Farthing wished to participate in this capitalist bacchanalia. A shopping spree on the docket, he snatched up the next taxi that passed and told the driver to make a beeline for Andorra la Vella's center.

Wandering along the Avenue Carlemany, Lord Farthing came upon a jeweler specializing in high-end diamond accessories. The glittering display case in the window set off lightning bolts in his brain – what Farthing referred to as one of his "moments of inspiration". It occurred to him that a diamond bauble of some sort might be exactly what he needed to impress a certain Lady Windermere, a young Countess from Hertfordshire whom he had attempted to charm – upon being introduced at a fancy-dress ball in London – by asking her if she perchance "came here often". This *bon mot* had helped distinguish him from absolutely no one, and he sought now a new pathway into her heart.

From his experience with the fairer sex, that pathway would most likely involve a heavy outlay of cash. This, Farthing had in droves, more than enough to indulge the object of his affection and afford a first-rate driver to defeat Buppy sometime in the future. He stepped into the shop and informed the gnomish proprietor that he intended to buy the most expensive diamond earring-bracelet-necklace combo in the place. On hearing this the proprietor nearly fell off his stool and sprinted about the shop in his haste to fulfill Lord Farthing's request, as if he were afraid the latter were intoxicated and might sober up before the deal could be completed. It was not more than a minute before he emerged from the back room with the *objets en question* artfully arrayed on a bed of black velvet, the effect being that of a miniature, more-dazzling Milky Way.

The proprietor looked to Lord Farthing with trepidation in his eyes, eyes which filled with tears as Farthing gave him the go-ahead nod. The jewelry was placed in a hand-carved, mahogany case with silver-gilt insignia and wrapped with silk ribbon, after which Lord Farthing was presented with the bill. Had he also been perched on a stool, there is little doubt he would have hit the floor like a lead weight. It was – befitting the Milky Way-like ensemble to which it was attached – an astronomical sum. But noblesse oblige prevented Lord Farthing from simply chucking the whole thing and hightailing it for the Spanish border. Woozily, he scribbled out a check and handed it to the proprietor, who kissed Farthing's hand and immediately closed the shop to go get drunk.

It was a decidedly gloomier Lord Farthing who made the return flight to London the following morning. Not only was he out two Renaissance paintings' worth of funds, but, as it turned out, attempting to bring in from abroad jewels the value of a small cruise ship delays one considerably at customs. An hour's paperwork and a hefty VAT tax later, he was finally on his way back to the old digs on Addison Road. The only thing that kept his spirits afloat in all this was the thought of Lady Windermere – she of coral lips and pale complexion – choking on her oatmeal when she laid eyes on the size of the rocks he'd purchased for her.

After swinging by Chez Farthing to drop off his bags, Lord F. headed straight to The Terriers to appease his rumbling stomach. The time was half-past twelve. Lord Farthing entered to find The Big Table filled to capacity and emitting a sustained cacophony of "Hear, Hear!"s and "Right, Ho!"s and various sounds of revelry. In the middle of the tumult he spotted Buppy, beaming like a Cheshire cat, who waved for Lord Farthing to come over. "There you are!" he cried.

"Here I am," said Farthing.

"I've been looking for you!"

"Here I am."

"Quite right, and late at that! Hurry up and tuck in! We're already two hours into the celebration!"

Lord Farthing accepted a gin and tonic with furrowed brow. "Celebration? What exactly are we celebrating?"

"My engagement, old man!" Buppy laughed heartily.

"He's gone and got engaged to Lady Windermere," said Sippy Thurston-Plank, a bit pink in the cheeks. "Can you believe it, this sheepfaced bleater?"

"Nothing to it," said Buppy. "I found out she was a racing fan, so I invited her along this past weekend to the Gran Premio in Monza. It's Sergio's home turf, of course, and dash it all if he didn't take the checkered flag. When she found out I was part-owner of his team, she was like putty in my hands." He raised a glass. "Cheers, what?"

Lord Farthing stood stunned a moment, then wearily raised his glass and downed the concoction in a single gulp. The warm burn in his belly did little to relieve his agony, but after repeating the gesture another dozen times he braced up a bit and was able to take the philosophical view. His Aunt Prudence was always going on about "kismet" and "fate" and how it's always at the height of one's revels that the universe beans you with a spitball from across the room. Nothing for it, Lord Farthing supposed. Lady Windermere wasn't such hot soup, if one thought about it long and hard. She sagged a bit about the neck, rather like a basset hound, and her left eye, while not exactly lazy, possessed a less-than-Protestant work ethic.

Perhaps old Buppy had done him a favor, saving him from a life of matrimony. It was like that old quote about clouds and silver linings. All in the way one looked at things. Lord Farthing preferred looking at things through the bottom of a tumbler. "Cheers, Buppy!" he cried, and tilted back his glass.

Part III. Writer's Block

Half past seven, and already the sun illuminated every crook and crevice of Oakley Manor's yawning estate. It had been the sort of morning that went from night to day as if a switch had been flipped, skipping dawn altogether, as if to say, "Well, here I am, now bloody well get on with it."

Adequately shamed, Lady Cresson had risen early and sat now at the small dining table on the terrace outside her bedroom, revising the notes for her memoir-in-progress, *The Amazing Floating Flapper*, which detailed her achievement of becoming the first woman to traverse the whole of Africa (north-south) in a hot-air balloon. It was a working title, suggested by a young junior editor at Huffington, Wyckombe & Gray, the London-based publisher who had purchased the rights to Lady Cresson's story. To call it the book's tentative title would be to dignify it beyond all bounds of reason, for as sure as Lady Cresson was about anything in this unfamiliar process, she was sure she would sooner spend another two weeks floating above Africa in a blasted wicker basket than see that horrid appellation affixed to her book.

She put down her pen and took a sip of tea, the warm, bitter brew like a salve on her parched throat.

Writing was a torturous process, she had learned. A month in and still she was stuck on drafting an outline. Her publisher's inquiries as to her progress were already taking on an insistent tone, something between a polite nudge and thinly veiled threat. Such was the lot of a tabloid darling. Right now she was big news, on everyone's lips, but in no time her stunt would be forgotten and someone else's name would be hogging all the ink. No doubt that would suit the rest of her family just fine, as the last thing any sensible nobleman or woman wanted was their name in the papers. To her publisher, however, every day that passed was money down the drain. The time to capitalize was now, and everyone who was anyone wanted a piece of the action. There was even talk of a film, with Lady Cresson to be played by Clara Bow.

Lady Cresson suspected her writing might be further along if not for the fact she found the whole affair rather ridiculous. What was there, really, one could say about floating over Africa in a balloon? It was much the same as floating over England in a balloon. The sun was more severe, surely, and the vegetation different. On one occasion she had spied what she believed was a zebra standing half-hidden in the tall grass, staring at absolutely nothing. Beyond that, it was a lot of eating and sleeping and relieving oneself in a most immodest fashion. This last part Lady Cresson meticulously omitted from her recounting of the journey. Neither did a single reporter ever question her about it, a fact that belied – in Lady Cresson's estimation – a stunning lack of imagination amongst the journalistic class.

Her publisher was adamant the word "flapper" appear in the book's title. So too did the newspapers push the feminist trope, placing Lady Cresson and her exploits at the end of a continuum stretching back through Louise Brooks and Lois Long all the way to Emily Wilding Davison and the Suffragettes. What any of them had in common was beyond her, except that they were all women who had done something other than marry or give birth to a child.

In Lady Cresson's case it was debatable whether she had met even those modest guidelines, as she had not been the one piloting the balloon. That task had been undertaken by a rather dashing flight lieutenant of the RAF named Reginald Greaves. The tabloids seemed particularly interested in this angle, one reporter going so far as to ask, with an implied wink, whether she found that altitude enhanced the pleasure of "barney-mugging". Jazz journalism at its worst.

In truth, Lady Cresson would have liked nothing more than a roll on the wicker with young Greaves, but the latter barely acknowledged her existence, spending the majority of the trip with his elbows propped on the edge of the basket, peering out towards the horizon. A sad, tragic air hung over him, compounded by his silence; he only spoke when spoken to first by Lady Cresson, and then kept his answers as short and to the point as possible. Once, when loneliness had gotten the better of her, she had ventured to pry into his personal life, how he had ended up in a balloon with her halfway across the world. He told her that he had been assigned to her as a reward for exemplary service in Iraq. Intrigued, Lady Cresson had pressed him for details of Babylon and the ruins of Hatra.

"I wouldn't know about any of that," he said, lapsing back into silence.

Lady Cresson felt her face turning red. "You must find all this rather silly," she said.

Flight Lieutenant Greaves busied himself adjusting the burners. If he had heard Lady Cresson, he gave no indication.

Lady Cresson shuffled through her notes again, attempting to get a handle on her progress so far. This did not take long, as she had only managed to fill three pages. "Brainstorm," had been the advice of her editor, and she had listened, scribbling down every random thought, musing, observation, and recollection the moment it came to her.

Sifting back through her mental detritus, now, she found herself even more despondent than when she had first sat down to a blank sheet of paper. She had, as far as she could tell, succeeded in detailing the entirety of her trip in just under a thousand words. That included her internal monologue. Proust might think a million words while staring at a madeleine, but for Lady Cresson, "cookie" would just about be the long and short of it.

There was nowhere to go from here. Even how to structure the book was a mystery.

Chronologically? "Day three – much the same as day two. Day four – etcetera."

Embarrassing as it was to admit, Lady Cresson could not explain why she had even made the trip. It was only now, when tasked to chronicle it, that she bothered to consider her motivations in undertaking such an arbitrary and unnecessary journey. Why a balloon? Why Africa? She looked down at her notes again, as if the answer might lie somewhere in those Delphic scribblings.

Down below on the lawn, Lady Cresson's youngest sister, Nora, was playing fetch with their pet corgi, Watson. Lady Cresson put aside her notes and watched for a while as Nora repeatedly threw a tennis ball over the diminutive dog's head. Watson would turn and scamper after it with all the verve and purpose of a cavalry commander charging the enemy's line. The sight of those stubby legs, barely long enough to lift Watson's belly off the ground, scuttling across the grass made Lady Cresson giggle. Each time he retrieved the ball and brought it back to Nora, she would hold it aloft, at which time Watson would spring to attention, leaning back on his haunches and fixing the ball with an iron gaze, as attentive and earnest the fiftieth go-around as he was the first.

Lady Cresson hadn't noticed Nora emerge from the house. It only occurred to her then that breakfast must have been served and cleared already. She leaned into the bedroom and checked the clock – a quarter past nine.

Nearly two hours had passed since she'd woken and all she had accomplished was to shuffle her notes a few dozen times. By ten o'clock she would have to begin getting ready. Her family had been invited to dine that evening at Chatsworth Abbey by the Dowager Duchess of Norfolk, whose son, the Duke of Norfolk, was – as Lady Cresson's father repeatedly reminded her – unmarried.

Lord Cresson was determined to see his daughter and the Duke wed. "If your exploits haven't already ruined our chances," he had said to her. He was dead-set against the book, convinced that the added exposure would only drive the Duke away. The truth was exactly the opposite; it wasn't until her name started appearing in the papers and on the lips of every high-society gossip in the country that the Duke had really taken notice of her. Her father assumed the Duke was a man like him, averse to scandal and public attention, but the younger generation were a different sort, with their own mores and attitudes and, what's more, their own lines of communication. Young nobles talked. Lady Cresson was well aware that the Duke had fallen in love with her. This had been confirmed by no less than five different sources, all of whom were in regular contact with him. The bigger question, the one that nobody had bothered to ask, was did she love him?

Stepping back out onto the terrace, Lady Cresson watched as Nora took her tennis ball and led Watson in through the kitchen door. Gathering up her notes, Lady Cresson went inside as well. Nothing productive would get done in these last forty-five minutes, she knew. Better to use the extra time to prepare. She languished some long while in the bath, savoring its warmth and the billowing steam that seemed to cleanse her mind of ill thoughts.

Afterwards she donned her silk robe and sat before the vanity so that her lady's maid might help her, as her mother phrased it, "put on her face". Lady Cresson watched her transformation in the mirror, still in awe after all these years at the poised and proper woman who appeared before her when the finishing touches had been applied.

The dress had been laid out the night before, a French voiles in cream, the hemline cut just above the knee. Once dressed, she dismissed her maid and set about adding a few, final accessories. She combed through her jewelry boxes, settling at last on a pair of Oriental pearl earrings that dangled just so and subtly reflected her dress's warm tones. From the hundreds of pairs of earrings she owned, she knew immediately they were the perfect one. In these matters, at least, there was no confusion.

Prudence and the Malnourished Soul

Throughout all the days leading up to that day, the eve of his forty-second birthday, Jonathan Quay had lived a thoroughly inauspicious life, the detailing of which would exhaust the patience of even the most duty-bound reader. Suffice it to say that like the vast majority of God's children his was a life built chiefly of routine, interspersed with the brief, superfluous moments of pleasure that in old age take the place of new experiences and ease us into our graves. Why on this day, of all days, it suddenly became clear to Jonathan Quay that his soul had been lacking something of fundamental importance is one of those mysteries the mortal mind would do better not to ponder too deeply, chiefly for want of any suitable answer. Why was Jesus Christ born on a Thursday, after all? He simply was.

Jonathan Quay was an exemplary model of all the things modern society cherishes. Not once in his forty-two years can he be said to have taken an incautious step, for Prudence was his creed and Recklessness the Devil's gilded deception. It had impressed itself upon him at an early age that money can be lost as well as won, and an open heart was but a target for Fate's fiery arrows. From the beginning he had charted a course far from the rocky shores. His eulogy – "He lived a long, practical life" – had been penned with one foot still in the cradle and was the perfect distillation of all that he had done and been. A curious religion, Jonathan Quay's, whose foundation was the very absence of Faith.

With such a philosophy as his guide, the circumstances in which Jonathan Quay found himself as he entered middle-age were not to be wondered at. His wife, two years his junior, was named Sandy, and to label her "plain" would be to confer on her a personality, something she decidedly did not possess. Jonathan did not love Sandy, for love was an emotion he was incapable of feeling and she incapable of inspiring. He did, however, care for her deeply and respect her as much as any woman he had ever known. She, for her part, shared his daily toil without whine or whimper, and if she had ever aspired to anything beyond quiet dinners at six o'clock and a crossword puzzle before bed, it had died out by the time she met Jonathan.

Jonathan and Sandy had one child together, a boy of eight named Herbert. Two memories stood out above all others whenever Jonathan thought about his son. The first was the day of his birth. Jonathan remembered the first time – after the umbilical cord had been cut and the baby cleaned off – taking his son in his arms, a tiny bundle wrapped in blue. A flutter had passed through his stomach and a warm contentment enveloped him like a shroud and conferred upon him for the rest of the day a grace one would have thought far above his attainability. He remembered wondering at the time whether this wasn't the boundless love a father was supposed to feel for his child, but years of reflection had shown it to be nothing so noble, only a heightened form of relief at having obtained the last of his middle-class aspirations.

The second memory had not yet had time to gather dust, the incident from which it stemmed taking place less than a year earlier. Walking Herbert to school in the morning, Jonathan had let his attention wander for a moment (he was often accustomed to daydream) when Herbert had taken it upon himself to cross a busy intersection, stepping right into the path of a speeding car. Without thinking Jonathan had rushed into the street and pulled his son to safety a mere instant before the boy was struck. As he sat down on the curb, panting with the aftereffects of adrenaline, his mind played out the gruesome alternative, the "what might have been" had he acted but a second later. A raw nothingness took hold of his stomach and held him dumb and mute for several minutes, so that in the end it was Herbert who was forced to don the mantle of maturity and comfort his stricken father. Looking back on this moment, Jonathan could not help but feel that he had been on the right track somehow, that this curious emptiness which had now come upon him like a thief in the night was due to a lack of something that had existed there on that street corner in those fateful moments when the world had ceased to be the orderly, predictable system he had once thought it to be. But a more concrete connection he could not uncover, his mind better suited to problems financial than those emotional and spiritual.

Jonathan Quay worked as a fund manager at a medium-sized investment firm in the city. His office, tucked away in the corner of his firm's ten-story corporate headquarters, which was itself tucked away into the corner of a recently built industrial park, commanded a view of the neighboring office building (a manufacturer of semi-conductors, he believed it housed); a small slab of parking lot, which seemed to be perpetually two-thirds full; and beyond that, an expanse of poorly manicured grass, stretching in softly undulating, greenish-brown waves to a point beyond his field of vision. This view had been his constant companion for the past five years, when his last promotion has raised him from the ground floor into the rarified air of middle-management. His position in the company, it was generally thought, was exactly where it ought to be for a man of his years and contributions, and if all went according to plan it was supposed that he would join the lower executive ranks sometime before his fiftieth birthday.

Jonathan understood his job well, invested for the long-term, and never failed to make for his clients a modest gain. "Now that the Fed has a handle on inflation, a safe bet's a safe bet." This was a phrase he had first spoken at a party over four years ago, and he had liked the sound of it so much that he continued to repeat it whenever he found himself in the presence of unfamiliar company, imbuing his voice with greater and greater meaning each time he uttered it, as if he had hit upon some grand and noble truth. And if it failed to make any kind of a first impression, it was never met with anything but respectful nods and polite smiles. This was a compromise Jonathan Quay could accept.

Jonathan's birthday celebration was to be a modest affair, dining out at a local restaurant early in the evening and returning home later for ice cream and presents. Only Sandy, Herbert and he would be in attendance, this not being one of the eight yearly occasions that necessitated the presence of extended family.

Though he dare not say it aloud, Jonathan was grateful for the impending intimacy, his more distant relations filling him with a sense of discomfort that bordered on consternation. How unlike him they were! Cousin Eddie, downing tumbler after tumbler of hard liquors well before sundown, and having the bad taste – at Grandmother Hazel's ninetieth birthday party, no less – to stroke a champagne flute in such a manner as to suggest the aroused male member. His oldest niece, Dawn, who at thirty years of age had visited more than forty countries but had yet to hold down a single, real job. ("What's a real job, anyway?" she had asked him on one occasion. "One with a comprehensive benefits package," he had retorted, wittily.)

How it was these people stumbled and floated from day to day doing exactly whatever they pleased, with no concern for the consequences of their actions, was one of life's great mysteries to Jonathan. It seemed to him that consequences were a necessary (and welcomed) constraint, the boundaries that gave form to one's existence. Without them to focus and guide one's energy a person might find themselves drawn in a thousand directions at once, spread so thin their very essence would dissolve, like a vaporous mass dispersing across the enormity of the universe.

Jonathan Quay awoke the following morning and was forty-two. This affected him in no discernible way. He felt much the same as he had the day before, had expected to feel thus, and the exactness with which Life had endeavored to meet his expectations depressed him to no end. Had his waking played out as a scene in a film, overlaid with mournful chamber music and with the camera slowly zooming in on the frozen blankness of his face, one would be forgiven for thinking that some profound realizations were taking place deep within his mind. But Jonathan, being on the most intimate terms with his own thoughts and feelings, had no such cinematic veil with which to delude himself. For this was the real world, inelegant in every aspect, and blankness was blankness, and the shrill cawing of a crow outside a vulgar substitute for Beethoven's *Sonata No. 14*.

Jonathan was alone in his bed. Sandy, he knew, was already downstairs preparing for him a special birthday breakfast of two eggs (over easy), two slices of Canadian bacon and an English muffin, the same meal she had made for him on each of his birthdays for the past eleven years.

At the foot of the bed lay a folded sheet of paper. Jonathan leaned forward to retrieve it and found it was a handmade birthday card from Herbert. "Happy Birthday Dad!" it said on the cover, a sentiment Jonathan found repeated, word for word, when he opened the card to look inside. He read these words again and again and - finding little more in them the tenth time than he had the first - set the card aside and dragged himself to his feet. Wearily, he shuffled over to the window and drew open the blinds on a gray, rainswept morning. For a moment he allowed himself the indulgence of imagining the scene as a metaphor for his troubled soul. But vanity did not come easily to him, and there was little about him that could truly be described as "troubled".

In a wrapped box, hidden away in the back of the downstairs hall closet, was a mulberry-colored bathrobe that was to be Jonathan Quay's forty-second birthday present. He had spied it accidentally a week earlier, stashed away beneath the bed, before Sandy had had a chance to wrap it. It was, he considered, a suitable gift, he having expressed a fondness for the garment approximately a month earlier during the course of a visit to a local shopping center.

Opening the bedroom window, Jonathan craned his neck to look out across the yard, then down at the glistening gray of the sidewalk stones below. His bedroom was on the third story; it looked, he thought, to be a long way down. The rain fell in a steady drizzle on the back of Jonathan's neck. He stood that way for some time, until a chill, like a ghost's icy finger, traveled down his spine and roused him from his thoughts. He leaned back into the room, closed the window and examined his pale reflection in the glass. With a rocky grimace and the piercing shriek of the tea kettle calling him from the kitchen, Jonathan Quay chose the more subtle form of suicide and headed downstairs to take his meal.

The Penitent Life

Mr. Farthingale awoke to a freezing cold room and the overwhelming suspicion that life was meaningless.

Whether this was a deeply held conviction or merely a product of his current circumstances was difficult to say. What little warm air existed in the room had been carefully harvested and stored beneath his heavy down comforter over the course of the previous night. He was loath to pull it back. The predatory chill of early winter circled round him like a school of sharks, awaiting just such an exposure.

But there were chores to be done. Goodness, were there chores! Mr. Farthingale could think of nothing more grotesque than to be faced with chores on a cold, gray Saturday morning in early winter. If only he had had something with which to brace his spirits – a decent night's sleep, or a lit and glowing stove, or even a warm cup of coffee waiting beside him on the nightstand – he might have been able to face the day with, if not exactly vim and vigor, then at least a sort of neutral resignation, a lack of bitterness towards life and the hand it had dealt him. As it was his situation was nigh unbearable. He lay like a paralytic staring at the ceiling of his bedroom, wondering how he had ever gotten himself into such a mess.

The cover was back. Mr. Farthingale had done it himself, almost without knowing. It was a reflex he had developed long ago out of necessity, lest he one day think too long on the merits of not getting up, of staying wrapped forever in downy warmth and the rest of the world and its chores be damned.

Much as he expected, the cold air moved in for the kill. Mr. Farthingale was prompted to action. He started sharply, then shivered, before pulling himself upright on the bed. With his feet dangling over the side, he groped around for his slippers, cringing whenever he missed and his toes made contact with the bare floorboards, which at this unfortunate hour had all the aspects of a sheet of ice. At last, his skin grazed something soft and warm and altogether more forgiving; Mr. Farthingale sighed as his feet slid inside, feeling something like relief that this first and most difficult hurdle had been cleared.

He could now stand up. He did so and almost immediately reeled. The cold buffeted his upper-body, which unlike his feet was ill equipped to deal with such an assault, and teamed with his still-drowsy condition to rob him of balance. He stumbled about the room in a herky-jerky fashion, like a marionette operated by over-caffeinated hands.

Draped across the armchair in front of the stove, in the opposite corner of the room, Mr. Farthingale spied his robe. He made a dash for it. He had occupied the chair the previous night so as to do some reading before bed and had foolishly forgotten to bring the robe with him, the crackling fire at the time lulling him into a false sense of security as concerned his own warmth. Snatching up the garment, he found the armholes and squirmed his way inside, only to leave out a terrifying yelp. Like everything else in the room his robe had not been spared the night's ravages. It was every bit as cold as the floorboards. Colder, even, if that was possible. Mr. Farthingale grit his teeth and proposed to wait it out, knowing that this punishment was only temporary, a penance before the salvation his own body heat and its silk wrapping would eventually provide.

What diverted Mr. Farthingale's attention and helped ease this painful process was the question of how the robe should have gotten so cold in the first place, situated as it had been directly in front of the stove. He shuffled over to the antique apparatus. Taking up the pair of tongs that dangled from a hook on the adjacent wall, he removed the lid and peered down inside. Lo and behold, two full logs, barely singed, remained in its cast-iron belly. The fire had died prematurely. More than ever, Mr. Farthingale gave serious heed to the idea of purchasing an electric radiator. Perhaps to modernize wasn't always such a bad thing, if it could rid him of the blasted cold that tormented him each morning.

Modernize! The very word made his flesh crawl. It was synonymous with vapidity, shallowness, and degradation of morals. Mr. Farthingale believed he was existing in an age of unchecked raillery. He mourned this most acutely in the evenings as he sat before the hearth in his study, alone. In the mornings he often put forth this accusation to his charges, whom he suspected as some of the primary culprits in society's rapid devolution. His earnest pleas only led to mockery.

One had to wonder why he bothered at all, knowing the abuse that awaited him in his crusade. But then, as was already noted, there was something of the penitent in Mr. Farthingale. It was quite possible he welcomed the laughter and derision, saw it as cleansing him of some minute sin the rest of the world neither noticed nor cared about – a sin, perhaps, which existed only in Mr. Farthingale's mind, but which weighed on his heart like a thousand albatrosses and transformed his life into a morbid balancing act of guilt and self-flagellation. No, he decided, he would not buy a radiator.

Mr. Farthingale worked as a fourth-grade teacher at St. Lucy the Blind Elementary School. Though he loathed every second spent there, he much preferred it to his days off. Work, if nothing else, gave Mr. Farthingale a reason to get out of bed in the morning, and his particular profession allowed him the unique opportunity to address the problems he saw enveloping society head-on.

Many avenues exist in regards to educating youth, and the one Mr. Farthingale had selected was undoubtedly of those less traveled. He himself had dubbed it the "Victorian Way". Though the State had long ago outlawed his 'Eleventh Commandment' (a staunch length of hickory which had once been the leg of a nineteenth-century dining room chair; Mr.

Farthingale had come to agree with the State's decision over the years, being, after all, not without his progressive side), he still took a decidedly hard line when it came to discipline. Anyone caught talking during lecture was made to stand at the front of the room with outstretched arm and a piece of chalk placed in his or her upturned palm. For each time the chalk was dropped or the child's arm grew tired and fell, he or she was made to stay after school and write on the blackboard a hundred times a psalm of Mr. Farthingale's choosing. Penalties for cheating were even more severe, and required the child to remain standing on his or her head in a corner of the room until he or she had correctly recited the familial succession of Abraham, all the way up to, and ending no sooner than, Hezekiah. The fact that none of the children actually took part in any of these punishments or even paid attention to Mr. Farthingale longer than it took to fire a spit-wad at his ample forehead hardly mattered. What mattered was that the sin had been exposed. The child's shame lay bare for all to witness, and if he or she cared not to make amends it mattered little to Mr. Farthingale. He knew judgment would be meted out a thousand-fold more terribly and swiftly on the other side.

Mr. Farthingale left the bedroom and lurched down the hallway to the kitchen door. As he opened it and stepped inside, he noticed a large, grayish cloud had appeared and was hovering ever so intimately about his head. It was his breath. The kitchen was even colder than his bedroom had been.

The reason for this, he noted with dismay, was that he had neglected to close one of the windows, a window he had opened the previous night in a fit of rage, a fit of rage precipitated by the unexpected malfunction of Mr. Farthingale's washing machine, which had led him, after several hours tinkering with the engine of this foul offspring of the Modern Age, to rip out the offending gear and heave it with all his might into the front yard.

It took only a second for Mr. Farthingale to size up what all of this meant – he would have to wash his clothes in the sink, in the middle of winter, in a room with no heat. Such were the perverse and perfectly orchestrated pranks Fate played. Not that Mr. Farthingale believed in Fate. Fate implied a blamelessness in the ill that befell one. But no one was blameless. Life itself was a blot on His canvas, and to live the greatest sin of all.

Mr. Farthingale filled the sink. Taking up a sweater from the basket on the floor, he plunged his hands into the icy water. Pain wracked his joints, turning into a dull numbness that crept slowly up his arms, like a hand reaching up from the grave, as the weight of a thousand albatrosses lifted from his heart.

Randall DeVallance

Wasted Lives

It began at the bar, like most things. Sam had burst through the door talking gibberish, a gleam in his eye, and everyone there knew things would soon get ugly. There were six of us there that morning, slouched over our beers. Sam made seven. Come that evening we would still be there, and later still, when the bell rang at two in the morning telling us it was time to stagger outside and find our way home. That's the sort of bar it was. "Blue collar", you might call it, if you wanted to be charitable, though almost no one who drank there had a job.

The conversation turned to free will, always a bad topic for a room full of drunks. Manny believed we had it, in spades. I didn't.

"A man makes his own way in this world," said Manny. He lifted his glass as he spoke, as if making a toast. This from a man who had been on welfare five years running.

"Manny," I said, "who's to say the second you walk out that door a piano won't fall on your head and crush you like a bug?"

"A piano?"

"Yeah, a piano."

He thought about it a moment and shook his head. "No, no, because I'd see the ropes and the people on the street hoisting it up. So I'd know there was something above my head and take steps to avoid it."

"What if the person living upstairs already has a piano?" I said. "What if it falls out the window the moment you walk out the door and lands on your head?"

"How's a piano gonna fit through an apartment window?"

"You're missing the point!" I said, but by then I'd forgotten the point myself. We were all watching Sam. He was down at the end of the bar lining up shot glasses – six in all – in a nice, neat row. The bartender, some new kid who didn't know any better, started filling them one by one with tequila.

"Jesus, Sam," said Manny, "it's only eleven o'clock."

Sam shook his head like a wet dog, put his hands on the bar and hunkered down over the glasses. "Listen…" he said. Then he started tossing back shots in rapid succession, grimacing like a little kid choking down cough syrup. A few seconds later, all six glasses were empty. "Listen," he said, gasping for breath, "I'm going to be rich!"

A collective groan filled the room. Sam had been concocting get-rich-quick schemes for years. He shouted for us to listen. "This time is different!" he said. The plan was simple – after crunching some numbers Sam had realized it would cost $195 million to play every possible Powerball combination. The Powerball jackpot had just gone over $400 million. "That's a profit of $205 million!" He grinned ear to ear and pretended to dust off his hands. "Even after taxes, that's a fortune!"

"Sam," I said, "you don't have $195 million."

It was a strong objection. But Sam surprised us by having an answer. Reaching down beneath his barstool (a bit unsteadily, as the tequila was starting to take effect), he retrieved a manila folder and waved it in the air. "My prospectus," he said, and slid it down the bar for us to look at. We gathered round like a football team huddling up.

"You're soliciting investors?" said Rodney.

"That's right," Sam nodded. "I get a few wealthy individuals to pony up the cash, and I take a modest consulting fee of, say, ten percent." He beamed at his own shrewdness.

"Sam," said Rodney, "what's to stop these wealthy individuals from buying the tickets themselves and cutting you out?"

A flicker of uncertainty passed over Sam's face, brief but unmistakable, like the shadow from a passing car's headlights flitting through a darkened house. "But it's my idea."

"It's not proprietary." Rodney had been a chartered accountant once, in another life, and fancied himself an expert in business matters.

"You mean…" Sam's voice dropped. "They can just take it?"

"Just like that. I know I would."

Sam lurched forward, looking as if he had just ingested six shots of tequila in rapid succession. He braced himself against the bar. Then, slowly, his head sank down, and he buried his face in his arms.

"Hey, man, don't sweat it," said Manny. "For that plan to work you would have had to fill out 195 million of those slips in only a couple days. You'd need years to do that. So your idea was stupid to begin with."

Sam groaned. That's how it went at the bar; dreams were swiftly and invariably crushed. We took turns buying him drinks.

The new bartender was a wiry, watery-eyed kid straight off the boat from Kilkenny. One would assume he had seen his share of drunks. Still, even he had begun to question the wisdom of plying Sam with bottom-shelf whiskey. When an Irishman tells you drink is not the answer to the world's problems, it bears paying heed. In the end, though, it was the only answer we knew, and so we insisted on another round. The bartender relented. He was an illegal alien, he told us, working off the books, and if our friend went into a coma or dropped dead it was no skin off his back, he was headed straight out the back door.

There was reason to worry. Sam looked like a March snowman, decaying right before our eyes. We could tell this one had hit him hard. Sam might have devised a million schemes in his day, but some were more cherished than others, and it was clear that this one had been his crown jewel. The light had been there at the end of the tunnel and now it was extinguished.

It was tough to watch a grown man sobbing in his whiskey. Fletcher, who'd been quiet up till now, couldn't take it anymore. "Would someone cheer him up already?" he said. "Tell a goddamn joke or something."

Manny said he had one. "This married couple is on vacation," he said, "and they go to the hotel to check in. They take their luggage up to their room and shut the door. The woman's looking around and suddenly it hits her. 'Honey,' she says, 'this is the same room where we spent our wedding night! Isn't that ironic?' 'No,' says the guy, and hands her a dictionary."

"I get it," said Rodney.

"Well then laugh, for Christ's sake!" said Manny.

"It isn't funny," I said.

"That's because you don't get it," said Manny.

"Rodney gets it," I said, "and he isn't laughing."

"I'm not so sure Rodney gets it," said Manny.

"Sure I do," said Rodney. "The guy is a dick."

"No," said Fletcher, "that's not it. The woman is an idiot."

Manny fumed. "It's about the word 'ironic' and how it's commonly misused!"

"Right, by the woman," said Fletcher. "Because she's an idiot."

"Look, this isn't some hackneyed commentary on gender…" said Manny, before a loud, sawing noise cut him off. We all turned to see

Sam, the side of his face plastered to the bar, snoring violently.

"Well, it's unanimous," I said. "That joke was terrible."

Manny had his pride. He slammed his fist down on the bar and leapt to his feet. "I'll see you gentlemen tomorrow!" Before anyone could protest, he was at the door. We recoiled as it swung open, the sunlight pouring over us like God's judgment, striking us blind. There was a deafening crash and what sounded like a man's scream.

The door swung slowly closed again. There was a moment where no one spoke as we waited for our eyesight to return. Then we all looked at one another, as if simultaneously having the same thought, and rushed towards the door. Shielding our eyes, we stumbled outside, nearly tripping over the pile of splintered wood, split wire, ivory keys and human limbs that littered the sidewalk. Blood leaked from the bottom of the pile, spreading out in all directions like an advancing army that forced the gathered onlookers into hasty retreat. It seemed to never stop, staining the concrete and the soles of our shoes a deep crimson.

"Well, I'll be," said Rodney. He sounded like he was in shock. I didn't know what to say. I took a step towards Manny, or what used to be Manny. I peered down at him, then turned and gazed up at the top of the building behind me.

"Ah," I said at last, "French doors."

The Writer

Although there were still some things in which he tried to find fault – a comma in the seventeenth paragraph that seemed equally disruptive in its presence or absence; the inclusion of the term "vexation", for which he could not find a less pretentious substitute – it soon became apparent to William Edington that he had written the perfect story.

It had happened quite by accident, like most acts of genius, starting as little more than a side project to relieve the pressure of composing his third novel, *The Unhinged Gate*. It was not a long work, scarcely ten-thousand words all told. In his hands, the manuscript felt light and insubstantial.

Edington flipped back to the first page and reread the story from the beginning. He was relieved to find he had not been mistaken. All the earmarks of greatness were there, the universal themes expressed through a tightly constructed, personal narrative, full of symbolism, foreshadowing, metaphor, and vivid imagery, rendered with a poet's flair for language. Not a single line wasted. In his workroom, silent except for the ticking of the wall clock, he studied the fruits of his labor, no longer taking in the words but viewing the pages themselves, noting their thickness when placed together, running his fingers over the corners and reveling in the contrast of the print against the bright, white paper. Inside he felt cleansed, but fearful as well, as if a stiff wind might come and blow it all away.

His call to Emily was forwarded to an answering service, which informed him that she and her new husband, Gregory, were vacationing in the Caymans. Three years after their split, Edington's correspondence with his ex-wife had grown increasingly sparse. Bursting with an energy he had not felt in some time, he decided to see his story off personally. Fastening it together with a paperclip, he slipped on his boots and buttoned his peacoat before stepping out into the street.

It was the middle of December. The holiday season had begun its magical transformation of the neighborhood. Colored lights snaked their way up streetlamps like stripes on a candy cane. Storefronts bustled with intricate displays – stuffed animals, toy trains, packages, trees, and other, more exotic decorations competed for window shoppers' attention. Edington waved to a man hanging garland from the spout above the hardware store.

The mailing of the manuscript was nothing more than routine, the simple matter of purchasing a manila envelope and proper postage. Edington had expected more, somehow. The entire endeavor had taken only five minutes of his time, and now there was nothing left to do but return home.

Treading along the sidewalk, Edington delighted in the 'crunch' the snow made beneath his boots. He passed the Fountainhead Grille, where he had spent many late nights drinking and carousing in his youth. The front window, which stretched for half a block, had been painted, turned into a mural of a snowman driving a sled across the wintry countryside. Gripped by nostalgia, he kicked his boots clean and stepped inside to warm himself.

It had been many years since the last time he had set foot in the Fountainhead. The management had changed since then; it was much quieter than he remembered it, though seemingly cheerful enough. He ordered a beer and made small talk with the bartender, a man whose face he recognized but whose name escaped him. Discussing amongst other things the weather, the price of gas, and the outcome of a local election, Edington ventured to ask about some of the old timers, friends of his whom he had lost track of over the years. Each name he rattled off drew a blank reaction, and gradually the bartender drifted over to the sink to wash glasses, leaving Edington to finish his drink alone. He hummed along to a few of the Christmas carols being piped in over the speaker system before slipping from his stool and leaving quietly, his beer only half-finished.

When he returned home, Edington put water on to boil and rummaged through his refrigerator for something to eat. He decided on pork chops and took two from the freezer to thaw. When the kettle began to whistle, he removed it from the stove and prepared a cup of tea (six sachets, as was his taste), bringing it to the living room where he took in the second half of a college football game. Having nothing invested in the outcome, much of the drama was lost, and

Edington felt only a mild flutter of excitement as the home team kicked a last-second field goal to clinch their conference title.

When the meat was ready, Edington sprinkled it with seasoning and Italian breadcrumbs and placed it in the oven to bake. While he was waiting, he placed a call to his agent to alert her that his story was in the mail and would be there in a couple days. He received a tongue lashing for not faxing the document instead, but Edington simply refused to modernize in certain areas of his life and insisted on sending his stories through the post. He assured her this was the finest work he'd composed to date. She told him she would try for *The New Yorker* or *The Atlantic* first, but that he shouldn't get his hopes up.

When the pork chops had browned, he removed them from the oven and made up a plate, which included potatoes left over from the previous night's dinner and a small helping of sweet corn. This he took back to the living room, where he dined while watching a detective drama on one of the networks. Edington found the characters bland, the situations unconvincing. He had come to rely on his television more and more over the years, though it seldom brought him any sort of fulfillment.

The food, when it had settled, made Edington drowsy, and though he was an avowed tea drinker he decided an evening stroll to the coffee shop would be a nice change of pace. The sun, very low in the sky now, provided little warmth, and Edington was shivering by the time he had covered the necessary two blocks. An hour from closing time, the shop was empty except for its two employees, a young man and woman Edington guessed were less than half his age. Their faces betrayed dismay at seeing a customer enter so late, but to their credit they were never anything but courteous, and in fact became rather talkative as time went on. They each had seen him wandering past the shop on numerous occasions and asked him what exactly he did for a living.

When he told them he was a writer, they were enthralled. Was it exciting living the life of a writer, they wanted to know? Was he on the road often, meeting new people, seeing new places? Edington dispelled their more far-flung notions, allowing for the occasional embellishment when he felt propriety demanded it. Made giddy by the rush of caffeine, Edington inquired about the two young workers. The girl was named Amber. She professed a love of animals and planned on going to school to be a veterinarian. The boy, Jeff, liked fixing cars, and would start working full time at his father's garage once he graduated.

Before Edington could follow up with another question, Amber mentioned to Jeff a party taking place that weekend at the house of a classmate. Soon, the focus of the discussion shifted, and Edington found himself lost in a maze of unfamiliar names and references, thoroughly banished from the conversation with no hope of finding his way back in. He finished his coffee, saying nothing more except "goodbye" as he got up to leave.

Returning home, Edington turned up the thermostat and waited for the chill to lift from his bones. The apartment was dark now, but he elected to leave the lights off, instead lighting a pair of raspberry-scented candles that sat on the end table next to his couch. He sank down onto the cushion and opened the wooden box on the coffee table that held his pipe and tobacco. Packing the bowl tightly, he struck a match and held the flame close, feeling its warmth as the first traces of smoke entered his lungs. He sat there puffing for some time, watching the smoke curl and twist playfully through the candlelight as he tried to figure out what came next.

Provincial Minds

The Doctor had breathtaking eyes. Two teardrop-shaped orbs the absolute black of a dead universe, his gaze was both deep and pointed, as if through it passed an invisible line stretching outward past the farthest reaches of creation and inward to the infinitesimal depths of the self. His brows, straight and sharp, slanted upwards from the bridge of the nose to the temples and gave him the appearance of having just said something wry. It was on these merits, the perfectly random product of his particular genetic code, that his almost unchallenged authority in the town rested.

People visited the Doctor for advice and comfort, and rarely did he turn anyone away empty-handed. But just as rarely did he seem pleased to have company, for the Doctor was a busy man. That much was apparent from the mess of charts, technical drawings and half-finished equations scattered around the room, and the frenzied way he moved amongst them, a manic expression on his face, somewhere between a good, stiff caffeine buzz and utter despair. He also suffered, with an increasingly short supply of patience, the mangling of his last name, which some eight years of acquaintance had done nothing to impress in the minds of even his most frequent visitors.

"It's Greek," he'd say, after another failed attempt, followed quickly by, "Just call me Doctor Z."

Doctor Z was a self-styled Renaissance man. At the age of seventeen he became a certified chess master in the state of Oregon, the youngest in its history. Born in Eugene, he kept a "Go Ducks!" 1995 Rose Bowl pennant prominently displayed on the wall next to his sterilizing cabinet.

Throughout college he dabbled in medieval painting techniques and was a strict adherent of the Turnovo School. Though his grand design of painting the Holy Forty Martyrs re-imagined as Bio-Med majors hit a fatal snag between Saints Philoctemon and Theophilus, almost everyone agreed that the finished portraits presented a reasonable likeness of the tragic men who inspired them.

But perhaps the Doctor's greatest love was reserved for croquet, a game he considered infinite in its possibilities and all the better for its sound basis in Geometry. As much a raconteur as a man of science, many were the times he could be found regaling the patrons of his favorite pub, The Rusty Hinge, with the tale of the time he defeated the Earl of Southampton's nephew, Patrick, by a clean eight wickets.

These were the imposing credentials the Doctor brought to Brickbottom County to begin research on a project so secretive it was known to the general public only as "Project X".

With a name so obviously secretive as "Project X," it was no surprise that the Doctor and his work were the primary topics of discussion amongst the county's residents. Speculation ranged from the mundane to ideas so wild even the most fertile minds of Science Fiction's canon had yet to discover them. With his background in medicine, many believed the Doctor to be developing some sort of cure, a miracle vaccine that would rid their county once and for all of sickness, misery, and death. These devoted men and women began to regard him as a sort of savior, a messiah figure who had appeared one afternoon "on the outskirts of the Old North Road, as if materializing from dust," as one popular retelling would have it. They made frequent trips to the Doctor's waiting room, bestowing upon him gifts of Bundt cake and herbal tea.

Yet the Doctor was not without his critics. Quite the contrary, some of the most esteemed members of the citizenry would have liked nothing better than to see him fall flat on his face. They found him odd in manner and grotesque in appearance, but their strongest objections were reserved for his work, which – though they knew not its exact nature – they considered to border on the mystical, a sort of 'blaspheme-in-embryo'.

"Your moral compass is nothing short of quizzical!" the Mayor himself had blurted out at last year's Green Jacket Society gentleman's cotillion. Only the Mayor's wife had prevented a full-blown scene from developing, blaming the outburst on a batch of grape brandy that not had been allowed to ferment the required six months. While no one was particularly satisfied with this explanation – least of all Foams, the distiller, who retired to a corner of the ballroom to sulk – it did succeed in checking tempers long enough for the Doctor to gather his wits and take leave of the event before insults could escalate into blows. All the way to the door derisive whispers could be heard, the hushed and venomous voices of a crowd in the throes of judgment, hurling at him slanderous words. "Rapscallion!" they said.

Oh, the colorful bluster of provincial minds! The Doctor would have laughed at their simple natures if the stakes were not so dire. Most troublesome was his adversarial relationship with deep-sea fishing magnate Harlton Mewes, owner of the local, conservative daily *Brickbottom County Trumpeter*. "If this is Project X, we here at the Trumpeter can't help but wonder what went wrong with those projects attached to the first twenty-three letters of the alphabet," it wittily declaimed in a Sunday editorial. Mr. Mewes, it should be noted, was a staunch fundamentalist, a tenth-generation Presbyterian who did not cotton to men standing in a place of reverence reserved for the Almighty. "When Our Savior returns, you'll know it all right!" he told anyone who would listen, oftentimes adding a "Harrumph!" out of sheer consternation.

With such powerful enemies, the Doctor's demise was inevitable. One day, on leaving the grocery store after an unsuccessful attempt to cash an out-of-state check, he was nearly hit in the head by a sizeable piece of granite hurled from the window of a passing car. In case the intent behind this act was misinterpreted, a message, written on a sheet of college-ruled notebook paper, had been attached to the stone with scotch tape. "Leave town," it warned, "or we'll hit you in the head with a piece of granite!"

"Probably just a schoolyard prank," he said to himself, though his stoicism sounded specious, even to his own ears.

They finally got him coming out of his office on a sunny afternoon in late September. As he turned his key in the front lock, his face toward the door, the Doctor felt himself seized from behind by multiple pairs of hands. His wrists and ankles were bound with horsehair rope, and he was carried to the town square dangling from a length of hickory, like a pig over a spit. His captors wore white hoods and bulky robes to conceal their identities, but at least one of them, the Doctor noted, had a penchant for red Chuck Taylors.

When they reached the center of town, they ascended a small, octagonal platform, a hastily-built construction of particle board, which the Doctor could only speculate had been erected specifically for this very occasion. Made to kneel and remove his shirt, he was confronted by a tall, lanky man holding a thistle-branch whip who introduced himself as the "Chief Inquisitor," and whom the Doctor recognized by voice as Harlan Culpepper, the owner of the feed store over on Willow Bay Drive.

"Confess!" demanded the Inquisitor.

"Confess what?" asked the Doctor, which earned him an audible thrashing across his bare back. The Doctor complained that this stung quite a bit, especially where the thorns had happened to pierce through his skin, and the Inquisitor explained that that was rather the point.

It took seven continuous days of thrashings before the Doctor finally succumbed, passing on into the hereafter as silently and mysteriously as the legends say he arrived. The official cause of death was found to be dehydration, and it was only the quick administration of emergency Evian that kept several of his captors from meeting the same fate.

When the body had been disposed of and the eulogy delivered by the minister of Bascombe St. Baptist Church in neighboring Slocum Pines County (Brickbottom's own Presbyterian minister, under pressure from Harlton Mewes, had declined to speak), those in attendance marched *en masse* on the Doctor's office, determined to uncover once and for all the insidious nature of his abominable sciences. The key, which the Doctor had been in the process of turning at the time of his arrest, sat patiently in the lock awaiting their arrival. Never one to miss an opportunity for grandstanding, the Mayor elbowed his way to the front of the mob to deliver a short speech and delay the unveiling until a photographer from the *Trumpeter* could be scrounged up to capture him in his moment of triumph.

With the fanfare out of the way, the Mayor at last turned the latch and threw open the door. The crowd surged forth, pouring through the narrow opening like sand through the neck of an hourglass, baying and howling, their voices hoarse with the righteous cries of the victorious.

They stormed the outer waiting room and flung themselves against the door to the laboratory, the heavy oak splintering under the weight and fury of the mob. With a sharp 'crack', the door was ripped from its hinges. A triumphant cheer went up as they charged into the inner-sanctum, in which no one but the Doctor had ever set foot, and it was there that they first laid eyes on the truth behind Project X...

The cries stopped. Nobody moved.

"Well, I'll be," said someone at last.

"Don't that take the cake," said another.

"'Bout what I expected," said a third, who was known for affecting disinterest. The rest simply looked on in silence, pondering.

"What do we do now?" asked Mr. Flane, the pharmacist, who was due home for dinner in fifteen minutes and had no time for silent contemplation.

"We can't just leave it like this," said the Mayor, who had October re-elections to think of.

"Let's burn the house down," said the minister, a great believer in the cleansing power of fire.

"Isn't that a bit drastic?" asked the Mayor.

"Drastic times call for drastic measures," he said, sagely. "Besides, if we burn the house down it will be easier to pretend none of this ever happened."

Everyone agreed this was true. A five-gallon tank of gasoline was procured from the nearest service station and a book of matches from behind the counter of The Rusty Hinge ("The same ones he used to light his cigars," mused Higgins, the bartender, who had always been fond of the Doctor). When the structural beams had been thoroughly doused, the Mayor, with his usual pomp, struck a single match and tossed it with great flourish through the open front door, into the waiting room.

With a dull 'whoosh' the house was ablaze, as spectacular and sudden as a Roman candle exploding. The crowd stood hypnotized in the street, watching the orange-red flames licking the sky and the plume of smoke, black as a widow's shroud, curling up into the soft night. They remained standing that way for some time. Then, one by one, they departed for the warmth and comfort of their beds, the righteous mass slowly disintegrating, becoming smaller and smaller until soon there was no one left, and nothing, not even a memory, of the Doctor remained.

A Changing of the Guard

Hypothesis was the graying champion, and I was the young up-and-comer with spark and vigor. It was inevitable we should meet. The people loved Hypothesis. He was a good champion, a legend in his own time, but the people could smell blood, and deep within them stirred that nameless something that yearned to see the myth destroyed. There comes a time when people need to be freed from their heroes. Not that anyone thought I could win. They had chosen me to throw to the lions. I was their martyr, their sacrificial lamb, but I possessed the twelve-part maneuver the press had dubbed 'The Devil's Gambit,' and so was not afraid.

We met in the Eastern Regional Backgammon Semifinals at the Monroeville Expo Mart. A master's class table surrounded by bleachers surrounded by lights, I climbed through the ropes and heard the baying of a thousand sweaty dogs, salivating, clawing at each other, their madness fueled by the promise of massacre. During the day they were accountants and doctors and kindergarten teachers.

Hypothesis was already inside, leaning back in his leather armchair, a snappy Baroque number with nail head trim. Externally he was the picture of confidence, the unbending rock. But something was wrong. Something deep. Though he tried his best to hide it, it trickled out through his eyes and tainted his

179

movements – the twitch of an eyebrow, the clenched jaw. The crowd was too far away to see it, but not I – it was fear. A shiver traveled down my spine, and at that moment I knew I could do nothing but win.

Famed Italian backliner Dino Baggio served as guest announcer. As my name echoed from the loudspeakers in broken English, a mighty roar issued forth from the crowd. Here and there, a lone voice could be heard above the din:

"Parisian Backslider!" it said.

So I was called because of my ethnic heritage and defensive style of play.

From the first row, William 'The Irish Cobra' O'Shea looked on intently. The winner of our match was to be his opponent in the Finals.

I crossed the canvas to my own chair, a modest Louis XVI swan back, and sat down. Before the contest began, in a show of gentlemanly goodwill, I extended a hand across the table and bade Hypothesis to shake it. The latter considered my offer and refused.

"Well . . . " I deadpanned. "It seems as though I've been gammoned."

Hypothesis: lumbering, slow-witted, pushing his pieces around like an old man sorting change. I danced around him with ease, employing the Hara-Kiri maneuver with considerable success. The crowd watched with pity as his moves became more desperate, wild, swinging at invisible men and the ghosts of former acolytes who had found a new god. As the match neared completion, Hypothesis went so far as to invoke the Crawford Rule, a desperate ploy and a sad ending to one of the most esteemed careers in backgammon's history. Doubling cube or no, I cleared my home board before Hypothesis could bear off a single checker. The win was crushing and complete. The crown had passed to another.

As the world exploded into flashbulbs and the cries of the new faithful, I retreated to my locker room to wait for the auditorium to clear. How much time passed I can't be sure, five minutes or five hours, but what began as a cacophony eventually dwindled to a single, solitary voice calling out from the void:

"Arthur . . . ! Arthur . . . !"

It was Hypothesis. I returned to the competition floor to find him still sitting in his chair, staring down at the game board.

"Hypothesis . . . ?"

"Let's go outside," he said.

We stepped out through a side door, feeling a rush of air as the heat of sanctioned competition gave way to winter's brittle cold. Snow fell soft and Zen-like through the beam of a parking lot lamp. Hypothesis reached into his shirt pocket and produced a cigarette, lighting it as he leaned against the metal handrail lining the sidewalk.

"I thought you gave up smoking," I said.

"That was back in my playing days," he grinned. "Can't see as how it makes much difference now."

"You're retiring?"

He shook his head. "I'm being retired."

"I never meant for it to end like this."

Hypothesis took the cigarette from his mouth, his eyes cutting a hard line through the pavement. Smoke seeped from his nostrils in thick, blue tendrils, amplified by the subzero temperature. All at once, as if coming to some sort of decision, he raised his head and pointed in the direction of the valley. "You see those lights down there? Every one of those lights is a home. And in every one of those homes live people . . . good people, who work and pray. People who save their money trying to make a better life for their children. They toil day in and day out, and no one ever gives them a trophy or puts their picture in the newspaper."

I cocked my head and looked at the champ, unsure of what he was getting at. Hypothesis took one last drag of his cigarette before stamping it out on the sidewalk.

"You and I exist because of those people," he said. "We exist because in their spare time those people choose to spend their hard-earned money watching us play a silly little game. Do you understand what I'm saying?"

Our eyes met, and I suddenly felt a great weight, as if some unseen thing were pulling me down toward the ground. Hypothesis pressed his lips together and nodded.

"They're all yours now."

For some time after Hypothesis left, I remained standing at the railing, looking down at the ordered rows of houses. Their lights flicked off one by one as the hour grew later. Inside were plumbers and teachers and nurses getting ready for bed.

Moving through the center of town was a truck-mounted plow, clearing the streets of snow. I watched the fine, white mist arcing from its blade and thought about how different the world was going to be from now on.

Across the Sea

Probably the death of her father was where it started, but Janice would have pointed to her first time reading Robinson Crusoe. There it was on the page, in black and white – a world of tall ships and impossibly wide oceans, of faraway lands where matters of consequence occurred daily. It confirmed once and for all her suspicion that the world she knew – the yellow-sided house on a half-acre of grass in a small, Pennsylvania town – was not the real world.

Afternoons spent sitting on the front stoop, observing the somnambulant pulse of the neighborhood – the precise, linear pacing of the man across the street as he mowed his lawn, back and forth, back and forth; the bobbing of tree branches in the breeze; sparrows flitting amongst the grass; clouds drifting past like bloated bodies on a lazy river current. Everything was rendered in primary colors – the blue sky, the green grass, the yellow house, the red fire hydrant on the corner – which only further convinced her that this was not reality but a panel in a comic strip. She was never able to shake the suspicion that if she walked far enough in any direction she would find the panel's edge, and whatever lay beyond it.

Another thing Robinson Crusoe had taught her was that peril was not something to be avoided, but the essence of life. Imagine if he had listened to his parents, she thought, had taken the route prescribed for him and become a dull and dusty lawyer arguing contract law in some provincial courtroom. Books would never have been written about him. She wanted that more than anything, to be written about, her legacy preserved forever like an insect encased in amber. Janice knew Robinson Crusoe was a fictional character, but that did nothing to lessen her desire. Somewhere in the past there really had lived men who had done these things, whose exploits were so big and brazen and beyond the average man's scope of possibility that only fiction could believably contain them.

In the center of town, atop a marble pedestal garlanded with trumpet creeper and fenced in by hedges, stood a bronze statue of the great admiral, Philemon Rousseau. Janice spent much of her free time there, either perched on one of the nearby benches or making languorous circles around its perimeter, admiring the statue from different angles. A plaque at the base of the pedestal recounted Rousseau's exploits, including the sinking of the *CSS Baton Rouge* in the Monongahela River in 1864. Not that anyone who grew up there needed a plaque to educate them about their town's most famous son. It was put there for visitors who never came, part of a delusional plan by the chamber of commerce to promote tourism. The only tourist who ever came was Janice.

When she wasn't visiting the statue and imagining what it must be like to send a boatful of men to their graves, Janice liked to hop the bus and make the twenty-minute ride north to Lake Erie. She had been told many times not to ride the bus alone, but ever since her father died her mother's edicts had become more like formalities, issued as if to fulfill some contractual obligation between parent and child. If her mother wasn't away at one of her two jobs then she was either sleeping or staring dazedly at the television, letting her brain unravel. "Stay close," she would mumble as Janice headed out the door. "No riding the bus." To which Janice would nod and immediately run down to the end of the block to do just that.

Lake Erie was not the ocean, but to Janice the distinction was academic. Water stretched off beyond the horizon, a seemingly infinite mass of churning black waves that almost crippled her, so deeply did it make her feel her own insignificance. Especially when she trekked to the end of Presque Isle, a long, sandy peninsula arcing out into the water like a giant scythe, she could easily believe that she was on a desert island staring out to sea. The vegetation might be different – lots of Indiangrass and cottonwood trees – and the sand not bleached quite so white, but she felt solitude there, alone with the seagulls and the rolling surf. On those rare, clear afternoons when the sun shone unimpeded the water seemed to ignite from within and glow a shimmering turquoise. In those moments it could have been the Caribbean, and Janice imagined herself staring through Crusoe's eyes, out across the Atlantic, dreaming of England.

She was doing just that, sitting cross-legged on the sand and gazing out across the water, when she first noticed the ship. "Ship" might be too grand a word; in truth, it was a modest sailboat, big enough for two or three people, docked in a small inlet at the far end of the beach. Janice watched it bobbing in the distance, looking almost toy-like so far from where she sat. The midday sun reflected off its hull in a blinding white glare.

Did the plan come to her immediately? Could one even call it a plan? It was not premeditated in any sense. No consideration was given, no weighing of pros and cons. Like an automaton whose springs had been wound, she simply rose and started off down the beach, barely conscious of what was happening. As she came closer to where the boat was moored, she began looking for signs of an owner, but there was no one in the vicinity. Not even the swimmers ventured down this far, where the sand began giving way to marshland. By the time she reached the pier she was all alone, the only sound the soft splashing of the surf as it broke around the pillars.

Janice stood looking down into the boat's interior. She was searching for some clue as to who the owner was, but it was empty inside, not so much as a stray lifejacket lying around. Sitting down, she dangled her legs over the edge of the pier and gently lowered herself into the boat. It was either to her credit or detriment that she did not stop to ponder the decision, but she no more considered herself a trespasser than the gull perched on the tiller. Janice was not a sailor, but there was something intimately familiar about her environs. So much of her time had been spent reading stories of ships and seafarers that the situation she found herself in had an air of inevitability about it. Janice did not believe in destiny, but somewhere deep down she knew she was meant to have found this boat.

All her reading had not familiarized Janice with how to operate a rigging, but a few minutes fiddling with the ropes was all it took to get the sail raised. Once she had untied the boat from the dock it lurched forward, crookedly at first, dragged along by the current. Then a breeze stretched the sail taut, and suddenly Janice found herself skipping over the lake's surface like a perfectly tossed stone. The sensation was so exhilarating that it took her a moment to realize the boat was out of control, banking to the right in a wide loop that threatened to bring her crashing back into shore. She grasped the tiller and pulled it hard into her chest until the boat's path straightened, her anxiety receding with the coast as she headed out into deeper waters.

The shoreline shrank behind her until it was a thin, green line on the horizon; soon it disappeared altogether. All Janice could see, in every direction, was water. A primal, elemental joy took hold of her then, and she let out a cry of exaltation. She was alone in infinity, a tiny pinprick lodged between water and sky. The boat skidded on, rising and falling on the waves. Janice leaned over the side and let the mist play across her face. Every nerve in her body crackled with energy. She wondered if this was what it felt like to be truly alive.

Such heightened feelings could not last forever. Time passed – an hour, two hours, maybe more. Janice felt her eyelids growing heavy. Her muscles sagged. She yawned deeply and curled up on her side on the cushioned seats, exhausted and content. Her breathing grew shallow and fell in time with the waves as they lapped against the hull. The boat rose and fell more gently now, rocking her like a baby until she drifted off to sleep. When she awoke much later, it was into darkness.